TEMPTING THE MARQUESS
by Georgette Brown

Cover Design and Interior Format

TEMPTING A MARQUESS

Georgette BROWN

Chapter One

Regency England

"WELL, YOUR WICKED COUSIN DEIGNS to show, does he?" Mrs. Grace Abbott asked of her daughter, Mildred, as she looked across the ballroom at a gentleman who had turned many a head by his appearance.

Knowing the question to be more of a statement, Mildred, a practical young lady of four and twenty, made no reply as she fanned herself to keep from perspiring overmuch, which she was wont to do in crowded spaces, during uncommonly warm summer evenings, whenever she fretted, and if she should have on one too many layers of clothing. All four of these aspects conspired against her tonight, and the moisture would certainly ruin the many applications of powder her mother, declaring that Mildred's complexion showed too darkly in the summer months, had insisted upon.

As the occasion for the ball was Lady Katherine d'Aubigne's fiftieth birthday, Mrs. Abbott had also insisted Mildred wear the shawl that her ladyship,

Mrs. Abbott's esteemed sister-in-law, had gifted Mildred last Christmas. Mrs. Abbott never failed to consider how she might curry the favor of her ladyship, the hostess of the evening's soiree.

Mildred adored Lady Katherine, but for once, her attention was more fixed upon her cousin, the Marquess of Alastair. She had hoped he would be in attendance and had thought of little else on the carriage ride over. Yet, now that she beheld his tall and imposing form, her nerves faltered and she wondered that she had the courage to speak to him, though she had never before felt intimidated. She was not one given to asking for favors from anyone, let alone the marquess, but she was in some desperation tonight.

"I heard he had been dallying with some chit from the *bourgeoisie*," Mrs. Abbott continued. "I would have thought, once he had come into the marquessate, that he would forsake his rakish ways. It is a shame, for the former marquess was an upstanding man."

"You ought not speak ill of Alastair, Mama," Mildred said. "He has been quite generous in providing for my dowry."

Mrs. Abbot sniffed. "Well, it was the only proper thing to do as he can well afford it and the two of you are cousins."

Though her mother, whose older brother had married Lady Katherine, needed no reminding, Mildred replied, "Cousins by marriage only."

"Cousins, nonetheless."

"The marquess is under no obligation to assist us, even if his aunt married Uncle Richard."

"No obligation? We are family!"

Sensing that her mother was determined to see Andre d'Aubigne, the Marquess of Alastair, in poor light, Mildred offered no further comment. Nothing short of his lordship offering his hand to Mrs. Abbott's daughter would improve the woman's perception of him. If such a miraculous event as a proposal should come to pass, Mrs. Abbott would have gladly forgiven all his imperfections.

"I suppose your father should introduce George to your cousin."

Mildred stiffened at the name of her fiancé, an uninspiring and officious man. But despite their connections to the d'Aubigne family, Mrs. Abbott, being the fourth daughter, and Mr. Abbott, a fifth son with no entailment to speak of, could not be particular. Mildred had had few suitors since her come-out. With a figure slightly plump and a face more round than oval, she had only the brightness of her eyes and the shape of her nose to recommend her countenance.

"I doubt Alastair will stay long enough for introductions," Mildred thought aloud. She knew her cousin favored gaming hells over social gatherings of any sort.

Mrs. Abbott scowled. "Well, I shall have to find your papa and ensure that he introduces George as soon as possible. George is quite eager to meet your cousin."

"Yes, he is," Mildred affirmed. She rather suspected that, if they had not any relation to the d'Aubigne family, George Haversham would not have proposed.

She had made a grievous error in accepting

his hand yesterday. The proposal had come as a surprise, and she had convinced herself that she ought not fall into the same habits as her mother in refusing to see the better qualities of a man. She should be grateful that a man had offered for her at all.

But last night, sleep had eluded her. The prospect of marriage, and all the obligations that accompanied that institution, had roused desires that she had worked hard to suppress for the better part of the year. They were wanton, unbidden desires, and they persisted despite the shame she felt at not having had the fortitude to keep her virtue. Her discovery by one she revered had, surprisingly, set her at ease with these yearnings. Nevertheless, as her parents had grown more anxious regarding her prospects of matrimony, Mildred had resolved to keep her secret wantonness at bay.

But it called to her often.

As the night wore on, she began to consider that spinsterhood did not appear all that unfavorable next to marriage with Haversham. She did not wish to be a burden to her parents, but if she should never marry, she decided that she could find employment as a governess or a lady's companion. Lady Katherine would assist her.

She had first considered appealing to Lady Katherine but loathed to trouble her ladyship with her woes. As it would be most unseemly for her to call off the engagement, it remained for Haversham to retract his offer or fail to come to terms with the marriage settlement.

For that to happen, she needed Lord Alastair.

As soon as her mother had left in search of her

father, Mildred rallied her nerves, dotted her brow with her handkerchief, and prepared to speak to the Marquess. But first, she was beset by three of her peers eager to ask after her cousin.

"Which dance do you think Lord Alastair most partial to? Does he fancy cotillions?" asked Helen.

"Alas, I do not think him partial to dancing of any sort," Mildred replied.

"But he must dance!" remarked Jane. "There is such the shortage of men with so many off to fight Napoleon. It would be so very impolite of him not to dance."

"I think you overestimate my acquaintance with him, but I would hazard that he would wear the label of rudeness as easily as he does the label of rake."

"How is it you are even able to talk to him?" asked Margaret. "He always appears quite put out at being spoken to."

Mildred was tempted to say that the Marquess must feel sorry for her, but he himself would protest that his selfish nature would not accommodate so generous a sentiment as pity.

"Millie, will you not sing my praises to him?" Jane asked. "I *am* your oldest friend. Perhaps you can mention that Henry Westley has taken an interest in me."

"I should be a better friend by *not* calling his attention to you," Mildred replied. "Surely you know his reputation?"

"My brother said the Marquess came very near to a duel once," Helen noted.

"How exciting!" Margaret sighed.

Mildred looked across the room to where

Alastair stood talking to his aunt, Lady Katherine. Even without the dash of danger to his character, Mildred understood his appeal. Nearing thirty years of age, his masculinity matured, the Marquess was a handsome specimen of his sex. He enjoyed the sports as much as cards and kept himself in fine physical health. He had the same black hair that all the members of the d'Aubigne family possessed and a smile that could charm when needed. But Mildred found his gaze too sharp and that his lips tended toward a frown.

"He has left a fair number of broken hearts in his wake," she remarked, though she knew full well that nothing called to the fancy of her sex more than the potential reformation of a rake by a woman.

"Surely he will give more thought to marriage now that he is the Marquess," said Jane.

Margaret waved her hand dismissively. "In truth, I simply wish to flirt with the man. That would be plenty exciting for me."

The women giggled in agreement. Mildred smiled. If she had shared their sentiments regarding Alastair, she, too, would have thrilled to receive a smile or a dance from him. Alas, she was to marry George Haversham, and would never know that fluttering of the heart, that spark of excitement, when the object of one's affection comes near. But she was not yet ready to reconcile herself to a life of dullness. She would save herself from such a fate. But she needed the assistance of the Marquess of Alastair.

Chapter Two

HIS LORDSHIP LOOKED AT THE longcase clock on the far wall. Not ten minutes had passed since his arrival. He would stay another twenty minutes before departing for his favorite gaming hell.

"Surely you will give more thought to marriage now," Katherine remarked.

If his aunt persisted on such topics, Alastair resolved he would stay only five minutes more. It was sufficient that he had curtailed his hunting trip to pay his respects to his aunt on her birthday. Aloud, he replied, "And why should you think that, madam?"

"You are the Marquess of Alastair now."

Unimpressed, he said nothing, compelling his aunt to state the obvious.

"You will want an heir."

"If I fail to produce one, the marquessate falls to my uncle."

Katherine wrinkled her nose. "My younger brother is ill prepared to assume the title."

"He is a d'Aubigne. That suffices."

"I suppose if that is your view on the matter, you need never marry."

"I see no reason to add unnecessary concerns to my plate."

"You are fortunate you've no mother to fuss over your unmarried state."

"Do you fret, m'lady?" he asked, for his aunt was as near to a mother as could be had, his own mother having been lost to him when he was a small child.

"I do not. You should know I am *not* the *conventional* sort of woman."

He did indeed know, for it was his aunt who had introduced him to Château Follet, known also as the Château Debauchery, but he raised his brows nonetheless.

"It is not your bachelorhood that concerns me," Katherine continued, "but will you never care for anyone?"

"I protest, madam. I would not be here tonight if I cared for no one. *You* are the reason I am willing to tolerate this tedious evening for any length of time."

"As much as it warms my pride to know that you care for me, I would rather you not confine your affections to me alone. When I am gone, who will be left to care for you?"

He looked down at her ladyship, small in stature but large in heart, and with a willfulness that knew little retreat. "You do fret."

"I suppose I do. Your friends are no friends at all. You have estranged your sisters with your profligacy. You think the rest of the family fools.

If you do not find someone to care for, you will die a lonely, miserable old man."

"Madam, there will always be those who care for my title and my wealth. I shall never be lonely."

"Then you will be miserable."

"That I am willing to accept."

Katherine narrowed her eyes. "You think so now because you are at the height of vigor and handsomeness. You will think differently when the wenches are not so readily had."

"Is that why you married?"

"Impudent pup! My dear Richard, God rest him, was the better half of me in every way. I never thought I should find a man who understood me so well. If not for Marguerite Follet, I should never have met my Richard. Perhaps she could recommend a lady for you when you are at her château this week."

He recoiled at the idea. "Madam, I intend to spend my time at Château Follet suffused in depravity. The only mate I seek is for purely venereal purposes."

He was about to excuse himself and make for the card tables when Mr. Abbott approached with a young man who had styled his hair in long, soft curls, though they did not hide his prominent widow's peak. The many layers of his cravat gave him the appearance of a fancy rooster, and his cutaway coat revealed his large midsection and wide hips to no benefit.

"Lady Katherine, Lord Alastair," Mr. Abbott greeted. "May I introduce to you the gentleman who will be my son-in-law, Mr. George Haversham?"

Katherine held up her quizzing glass, and Alastair knew she was hardly impressed.

Haversham bowed. "A pleasure, Lady Katherine! Many, many happy returns on your birthday. May I compliment you on a delightful soiree? I look forward to the performance of the chamber quartet."

"Son-in-law?" she queried, and despite her poise, Alastair detected a hint of vexation. "When did this happen?"

"Yesterday, my lady, and my happiness is not lessened by the passage of a day," Haversham answered, his silly grin reaching from ear to ear. "Lord Alastair, may I compliment you on your generosity for supplying the dowry for Miss Abbott? Will you be participating in the drafting of the marriage settlements as well?"

"Good God, why would I?" Alastair returned. "Miss Abbott is not my daughter."

Mr. Haversham laughed as if he had been told a droll jest. "No, indeed! I merely thought, as you seem to be quite charitably supportive of your family, that you would extend your interests to all areas of concern. I certainly would not refuse you if and when you saw fit to intervene. Indeed, I should be honored by your involvement."

"My *involvement* extends only so far as providing Mr. Abbott the funds he seeks. What he chooses to do with the monies, even if he should choose to wager it all on horseflesh, is his affair."

Haversham's brow furrowed as he contemplated what it was the Marquess might be implying.

"I shall be forever indebted to you for your munificence, my lord," Mr. Abbott said.

The marquess expected the man knew better than to comment further or Alastair would be compelled to withdraw his donation. Millie was no dolt, and her intelligence had to come from one of her parents.

"Yes, yes!" Haversham nodded. "We are immensely indebted and exceedingly grateful for your kindness! I cannot give words to express how delighted I am that we shall all be family! Of course, the d'Aubigne name is an illustrious one, whereas I must claim a more humble background, but I think we shall deal well with each other. I should only be too happy to be of service, always, and your humble servant, etcetera."

With a frown, Alastair looked to Abbott to have the sycophant removed.

"Come," Abbott said to Haversham, "I think his lordship and Lady Katherine must have many other guests to greet."

"It was an honor to finally make your acquaintance," Haversham said with a final bow.

When they had left, Katherine turned to her nephew. "My goodness, how much did you promise Abbott?"

"A mere two thousand pounds," Alastair replied. "I thought granting him the sum would spare me his attentions, but I worry that is not to be the case. You had best advise your brother-in-law or I shall rescind my offer."

"I must say that this is perhaps the kindest display of benevolence I have ever seen you make. I am impressed. Perhaps there is hope for you yet."

"Madam, I hope not."

"It is a shame two thousand pounds could not

attract better for Millie." Her brow furrowed. "This is all so sudden. I wonder that she did not speak to me of this. I do not think he will suit Millie at all. Not at all. I am rather surprised that Abbott approves of this Haversham fellow. I think her mother and father worry that she will be doomed to spinsterhood if she does not marry soon. Still, I think they underestimate her qualities."

Alastair suppressed a yawn and glanced once more at the clock.

"It was kind of you to take an interest in your cousin."

Alastair felt the keen eye of his aunt surveying him. "If my giving Abbott two thousand pounds gives me the appearance of altruism or suggests that I give a damn what others are about, then I have made a grievous error. Ah, I see Mr. Priestly is here. He had asked me to invest in the purchase of a racehorse with him. Pray excuse me, madam."

"You will be off soon, I gather?"

"You know me well."

"I intend to travel to Bath within a sennight. I know the fashionable prefer Brighton or Weymouth these days, but the rooms at Bath are still in good shape. I should consider it a fine birthday present if you were to join me."

Alastair suppressed a shudder at taking the waters at Bath. "Recall that I am to spend three days at Château Follet."

"Of course. If I were years younger, I would certainly prefer Château Follet to Bath."

"I had commissioned for your birthday a

pianoforte from Vienna. I regret that its delivery has been delayed, but it will have a full six octaves."

"I appreciate the grandeur of such a present, but you need not have. You would make me a happy woman if you granted me something far less impressive but much more meaningful. I would ask nothing more of you if you granted me this one wish."

He raised his brows. "If it is in my power, madam."

"Choose for me one person whose concerns you will take to heart. One person to care for—that is not me. Do this, and I shall even refrain from ever troubling you with talk of marriage and heirs."

He frowned. "Who is to be this person?"

"It is for you to choose. You have many in your family whom could use your protection, guidance and wisdom. I am certain you will make a selection that will make me happy. And this would be the best birthday gift of all to me."

From the corner of his eye, he saw Priestly walking away. "Very well, I will give it consideration."

"Well, do not take forever to make your decision or it will not qualify as a birthday present."

He sensed that Katherine had more to say, but she knew better than to stay him too long. After speaking with Mr. Priestly, he would take his leave. There were too many mothers present who had set their sights upon him, though if they knew what he planned in the way of female companionship this weekend, they would reconsider him as a marital prospect for their daughters.

He had not been to Château Follet in some time and looked with anticipation to indulging in debauchery in the coming days.

Chapter Three

MILDRED HESITATED AS SHE OBSERVED her cousin taking his gloves and hat from the groom. He was taking his leave and would not be pleased to tarry. But if she did not speak with him now, she knew not when they would next meet. Resolved, she approached him.

"Alastair, may I have a minute of your time?" she asked, reminding herself that the frown he wore was customary and its cause need not be attributed to her alone.

He turned his dark and penetrating gaze upon her, and, as she had come to stand closer to him than she'd intended, she was quite conscious of how much taller and broader he was than her, though she was no petite maiden.

"My God, you look dreadfully pale, Millie," he drawled in his rich baritone.

A more mannered woman of society might take exception to such a greeting, but Mildred did not mind dispensing with the niceties. "I know it. Mother made me apply at least six coats of powder."

"It looks terrible. I would not recommend it."

"Thank you for your counsel, but I did not come seeking your advice on my toilette. Rather, I had hoped to have a minute with you—"

He raised his brows. "A minute?"

"A few minutes," she corrected as she fiddled with her necklace of pearls. "I know you are eager to attend your gaming hells and will not trespass too much upon your time."

He seemed slightly amused that she knew his destination. "A *few* minutes then, Millie, and only because I know you are economical with your conversation—an uncommon trait in your sex."

"I am much obliged, sir." Feeling the gazes of Helen, Margaret and Jane upon her, she delayed her own purpose for the moment. "I take it you will not stay for the dancing?"

His look of boredom was her answer.

"You would make many a woman happy if you did," Mildred said.

"I would raise many a false expectation," he returned.

"Do you know my friend Jane? I think Henry Westley takes an interest in her—"

"Millie, what is the purpose of our *tête-à-tête*?"

She took a fortifying breath and adjusted her pearls. "I have not had the chance to thank you for providing my dowry."

He groaned. "If I had known my provision would engender such a fuss, I would not have done it."

She perked. "Then don't."

He was taken aback, a rare occasion, for very

little surprised or even seemed to interest the marquess. "Don't what?"

"Don't provide for my dowry. I would rather you had not."

He stared at her as if looking for signs of madness.

"I am not yet ready to marry," she explained.

"But it is done. Your father introduced me to your intended tonight."

"And what think you of him, Alastair?"

"You have no wish to know my opinions. They are rarely ever favorable."

"They could not be worse than mine on this matter."

"If you don't like the fellow, why did you accept his hand?"

"Father impressed upon me that I had to. I was overcome, I think, by guilt and a sense of responsibility to my family—I am not you, Alastair. I cannot dismiss what others expect of me."

"I assure you that life is much simpler when you pay others no heed."

"I am quite certain that, without a dowry, Mr. Haversham will lose all interest in me."

His lordship let out a long breath. "Millie, this is not my problem. I have no desire to interfere in your family."

"I am not asking you to speak to father. Simply withdraw the dowry."

"While I may have granted your father his request in a moment of weakness, I will not retract my word. It would not be gentlemanly."

"Since when were you concerned with being a gentleman?" she cried.

He could not resist smiling. When he did, his eyes of grey sparkled. It was what had many a woman undone in his presence.

"Dear Millie, you are far too clever for that Haversham charlatan."

He began putting on his gloves. Seeing that he intended to leave, she suppressed the urge to scowl at him.

"Are you quite certain you wish to invite him into the family?" she tried.

Unperturbed, he donned his hat. "Your few minutes have come to an end. Good night, Millie."

She knew better than to try to stay him. And she was too vexed for words. She should have known Alastair, though he indulged her more than he did most others, would make no effort to come to her aid.

Chapter Four

"OH, LADY KATHERINE, IT IS beautiful!" Mildred remarked as the carriage came into view of the château.

Built in the early 18th century and laced with a baroque cornice, the structure had three stories with two pointed towers serving as bookends of the perfectly symmetrical façade. The steep hip roofs of zinc contrasted with the ivory stones. One would have thought the château plucked straight from the French countryside. It stood nestled among mighty oak trees and low verdant hills.

Her ladyship looked out the carriage window with a wistful sigh. "I have not set eyes upon it in many years. Not since Richard passed."

Mildred turned to Lady Katherine. "I cannot thank you enough, my lady, for asking me to join you."

"Careful you do not express too much gratitude or you will sound very much like your betrothed."

Mildred gave a wan smile before sighing. "Yes, though I shall be Mrs. Haversham soon enough."

Her ladyship shuddered. "If you were my child, and I do regard you as such since I have none of my own, I would not permit this marriage to happen. I advised your parents that Mr. Haversham would not suit you, but it appears he is entailed some property, and they feel you will be taken good care of by him. Nonetheless, I had hoped they esteemed me enough to take my recommendation."

"They regard you highly, my lady! But on this, they believe they have the approval of Alastair."

"Hm. And Andre refused your request?'

"He has no wish to concern himself with my troubles."

"Not even for his favorite cousin?"

"I hardly qualify as his *favorite* cousin. I am merely the one who vexes him the least."

"That is no small accomplishment with Andre."

Mildred returned to looking at the château. When Lady Katherine had suggested she take Mildred to Bath with her, Mildred could not have been more thrilled. She did not often travel with her family and had not been to Bath since she was a child. Besides the springs and bath houses, she recalled streets lined with shops, treats of all sorts, and brightly clothed men selling tonics that healed everything from fatigue to warts. But first they would stop to stay a night at Château Follet.

"There is something you should know about the château and its proprietress, Madame Follet," said Lady Katherine.

Mildred gave her ladyship her full attention. There was a peculiar gleam in the woman's eyes.

"It is also known as the 'Château Debauchery.'"

"The Château Debauchery?" Mildred echoed, amused and intrigued.

"The late Monsieur Follet was once imprisoned with the Marquis de Sade and the Comte de Mirabeau."

Mildred's eyes widened. "How wicked."

"Yes, wicked indeed."

"But you say you met Uncle Richard here?"

"I did, but Château Follet is no place for love. It is a simply place where men and women indulge their prurient desires, without the judgement and condemnation that society would render."

Mildred looked carefully at her ladyship to ensure she did not jest, though it did not surprise her that Lady Katherine would speak of such things. The two women had formed an unexpected bond after her ladyship had come across Mildred and the stablehand in a compromising way in the greenhouse. Mildred could not have been more mortified, certain she had ruined herself and her family. But, to her great astonishment, Lady Katherine had not castigated her. Instead, she had allowed Mildred to take her into her confidence.

"I shall not commit so dreadful and shameful an act again," Mildred had promised.

"Nonsense, child. You cannot quell the natural desires of your body," Lady Katherine had replied.

Mildred had never been so stunned in her life. Thus began an unusual rapport. Lady Katherine spoke to her of unmentionables, of subjects no proper woman would ever speak, not even to a sister. But Mildred, eager to learn, and relieved that her carnal cravings might not be so odd and reprehensible if a woman like Lady Katherine shared in them, drank in every word.

"Is it still known as the Château Debauchery?" Mildred inquired.

"More than ever, I think," her ladyship replied.

"And we are to stay here for the night?"

"*You* will stay here. I am far too old for the goings on of the château, and, without Richard, it is not the same. And you will enjoy yourself better without my company."

Mildred stared at Lady Katherine with eyes agog. "You are not staying?"

"Worry not. The guests are most discreet, and Marguerite—Madame Follet, that is—will watch over you. I will speak with her."

"But where will you stay?"

"I've an old friend who lives not far, and I mean to pay her a visit. I will return the morrow to fetch you."

Mildred felt the luster of her prior elation diminish. "I am to be alone at the château?"

"My dear, you are a woman after my own heart. I promise you will have a fine adventure at Château Follet."

"But I know no one. What am I to do?"

"Anything you wish. Madame Follet will acquaint you with all you need know."

"But where shall you stay?"

Still astonished and now discomfited, Mildred felt her mind in an unsteady whirl. Her ladyship placed a reassuring hand over hers.

"Do not fear, my child. Château Follet is wondrous. If you are to marry that Haversham fellow, you ought to grant yourself one last adventure before you are shackled to the tedium of marriage. Trust me, without Château Follet, as much as I loved your uncle, I wonder that our marriage would have lasted as well."

Mildred did trust Lady Katherine. She admired her ladyship's unabashed honesty of carnal matters and her knowledge of the libidinous. The consummation of the marriage was the part she most dreaded with Haversham. The man fumbled to kiss her hand and had a painful propensity for planting his foot atop hers whether strolling, dancing or even sitting. How could he possibly fulfill her corporal cravings?

The opportunity presented to her in Château Follet was rare and special. She pressed Lady Katherine's hand in gratitude.

"I had recommended Château Follet to another before," her ladyship said. "It did not disappoint. I think you will have a most memorable stay. Be free. Be bold. Be wanton."

Mildred glanced out the window and saw that they were about to draw up to Château Follet. It was a little petrifying, but she felt her excitement return. Even greater than before.

With equal parts apprehension and anticipation, Mildred followed Madame Follet through the Château. Madame Follet, though several years older, possessed a youthful vibrancy. Mildred had taken to her in an instant and felt she would have done so even if Lady Katherine had not extolled her friendship with the woman. Madame was one of those fortunate women whose beauty did not fade easily with youth. She was much what Mildred was not: stylish in her turban and Turkish shawl, fair in countenance and hair, and slender everywhere from her neck to her fingers. In contrast, Mildred had dark locks, almost as black as the d'Aubigne tresses, and a cherubic face.

"I have the perfect room for you here in the west wing," said Madame as they continued down the corridor. They passed by a room with an open door, and Mildred thought she saw a couple, both only partially dressed, upon the bed kissing.

Noticing the look of surprise, Madame smiled. "Some guests do not mind if others watch and observe."

"Truly?"

This was beyond anything Mildred had considered. It was...provocative.

"Would you like to watch?"

Her breath caught. "Pardon?"

"Being a *voyeur* can be quite titillating."

Mildred hesitated. She had not been here above an hour and had not thought to be thrown into the activities already. She had thought she would have more time to adjust to her surroundings, though she knew not how one would prepare for a place like the Château Follet. For certain, watching another couple in congress was extremely naughty. But her response came far more easily than she expected.

"Yes."

Turning around, they went back and stood at threshold of the couple's room. The woman, dressed only in her shift and stays, was lying upon the bed. The man, in only his shirt, hovered above her, kissing her lips, her throat, the top of her bosom. The woman arched her back, trying to press her body closer to his.

"Pray, tease me no longer. I must have you," she murmured.

Mildred stood as still and as quiet as she could, hoping they would not notice her. Her mind screamed that what she did was wrong. Nevertheless, warmth stirred in her belly.

The man straddled the woman, laying his hips over hers. There was a familiar thrusting motion, a sigh from the woman. Mildred felt the heat travel up her cheeks. Was she truly watching this? The man rolled his hips at the woman, who grasped his arms and alternated between grunting and gasping. Their brows furrowed, their cheeks flushed. A mix of emotions churned inside Mildred. She knew their pleasure, knew the corporal cravings that were being simultaneously stoked and satisfied. Thus, she felt as if she were sharing in their interaction. It was naughty to bear witness to such an intimate act, but it was a titillating sight.

The woman's gasps quickened, as did his grunting. His hips hammered into her ferociously. She gave a gasping cry. Seconds later, he roared as he spent before collapsing atop her. They lay, still entwined, breathing hard, their mission complete. Mildred did not move, but she did not know if she ought to stay. For certain, if they saw her, her face would ripen into a tomato.

Sensing her unease, Madame quietly withdrew

and Mildred followed. They continued down the corridor. Mildred was silent as she tried to calm the tumult inside her. She had enjoyed the scene, had envied the woman upon the bed. Would she herself ever be so bold?

"You are much like Lady Katherine," Madame said. "She, too, is possessed of an adventurous spirit."

Glancing at Madame, Mildred was filled with a sort of gratitude. For years, until that fateful encounter with Lady Katherine, she had thought herself a most depraved young woman. She knew no one she could talk to. Nothing seemed to stymie the wicked urges within her—not attending church, not reading the Bible over and over, not filling her days with mundane activities, nothing. It was truly a strange affliction because the satiation of it was ever only temporary. In the quiet of her own chambers, she would attend that craving by hand. But, time and time again, the yearning would return. And when she had given of herself to the stableboy, it seemed she had only unlocked an appetite for more.

"Here are your chambers," Madame said, showing Mildred into a nicely appointed and perfectly respectable anteroom.

No one would suspect anything untoward occurred between its walls. Even the pastoral painting upon the wall, of a woman entertaining the attentions of a man on either side of her, seemed tame. Mildred took in the rose-colored, printed silk and golden candelabras upon the walls, and how the late afternoon sun filled the entire room with light. The mahogany furnishings were finer than any in the Abbott house, but it was the general cheerfulness of the room that Mildred found delightful.

"I thought these chambers would suit you." Madame smiled. "As you have no maid of your own, I will have one of mine attend you. Her name is Bhadra. Supper will be at six o'clock. Till then, you are free to roam the château as if it were your own."

Madame gave her a parting smile. Mildred would have liked her hostess to stay. She would have liked to acquaint herself more with the woman, and how the Château Debauchery had come into being, but she would not keep Madame Follet from the other guests.

Alone, she opened the door to the bedroom to see a beautiful post bed clothed in fine linen. She grazed the back of her hand over the soft bedclothes before sitting down.

"Oh!" she exclaimed upon seeing her reflection in a large gilded looking glass above the fireplace. The glass was tilted toward the bed.

How very lecherous, she thought to herself with a smile. Giddiness percolated. She could hardly believe she was to spend the night here. Alone. A part of her wished Lady Katherine would have stayed but perhaps it was, as her ladyship suggested, better this way. Without reminders of her present life, she might lose herself more readily in the world of Château Follet.

She did worry what would happen if she should somehow be discovered here, but Madame Follet assured her that only the most discreet persons were permitted within the château's walls. Any breach of confidence resulted in a permanent ban, and the guests were too devoted to the freedom and opportunities afforded by Château Follet to risk expulsion.

"Some guests come as a couple," Madame had explained. "Others may find their partners upon arrival. I have many individuals who are unattached, and I know there will be a gentleman who would suit you well."

Mildred was not as confident as Madame Follet, though the hostess had named more men than women. If she were not selected, should she take her leave?

"Nonsense," Lady Katherine had replied. "I do not intend to return to collect you till noon the morrow. And I expect, when I return, to receive a rousing account of your time here."

Mildred was, therefore, stuck. It had even seemed to her that Lady Katherine had been in some hurry to leave the château.

Unbuttoning her spencer, Mildred lay back upon the bed and looked at the painted ceiling. Naked cherubs gazed down at her. Her mind wandered back to that other room, to the man rutting atop the woman. The heat between her legs had not completely dissipated.

Slowly, she pulled up her skirts and reached between her thighs to find that little bud of sensation. Replaying the memory of the couple, she sighed as she stroked herself. Yes, she would have liked to be the woman below his bucking hips.

The sound of the door opening made Mildred jump off the bed.

"Miss Abbott?"

It was the maid. Composing herself, Mildred entered the anteroom to find a lovely young Indian with hair of ebony and large almond-shaped eyes.

"You must be Bhadra."

"Yes, miss. Your effects are being brought—ah, here they are."

A groom came up behind her and set down a trunk and portmanteau. He was rather a handsome fellow, Mildred thought to herself, wondering if the servants took part in the château's activities. If she could not find a partner among the guests…

"Shall I dress you for supper, miss?" Bhadra asked.

Mildred marveled at the peaks and valleys of the maid's intonations as she spoke.

"I've not an impressive wardrobe," Mildred said as Bhadra opened the trunk.

"Fine clothing is hardly necessary here, miss. Some guests go without clothing at all."

Mildred imagined what it might be like to walk about in the buff. She had not the confidence to do such a thing but was impressed there were those who would. She wondered how she would react if she came across a nude? How did one stop oneself from staring?

"Even at supper?" Mildred asked.

"Not the first night, lest Madame requests it so."

Mildred faltered. She could not conceive of sitting down to supper sans clothing. How could one concentrate enough to eat? She hoped Madame would not make such a thing mandatory. Mildred would not mind if others wished to shed their garments, but she had no desire to parade her nakedness. If she had a body worth revealing, she might feel differently. Instead, her thighs were a bit wide in proportion to the rest of her legs, there was a tad too much swell to her belly, and she would have preferred a less buxom bosom.

With Bhadra, she undressed from her traveling clothes and selected her finest muslin for supper, the same dress she had worn for Lady Katherine's soiree. It was a simple gown of white with lace at the hem and a lavender sash. In the spirit of the debauchery, Mildred wore only two layers of petticoat. Bhadra had laced her stays extremely tight and this caused her breasts to swell above the décolletage more than usual.

"Do you wish for powder?" Bhadra asked after finishing the coiffure, leaving a few tendrils to frame the face.

Recalling Alastair's comments from the soiree the other night, Mildred shook her head. After applying rouge to her lips, she looked in the vanity and was pleased with what she saw. She looked as pretty as Mildred Abbott could look.

"Monsieur Laroutte will escort you to supper," Bhadra informed.

"Who is Monsieur Laroutte?"

"Madame Follet's brother."

Monsieur Laroutte was at least ten years Madame's senior, but Mildred found the man captivating. They conversed in French, and by the time they had reached the dining room, Mildred decided she would be quite pleased to be paired with the man. However, after seeing that she was seated at the table, he sat at the end of the table opposite where Madame sat at the head, and began conversing with a superbly dressed gentleman to his left. By the manner in which the two men exchanged glances and leaned toward each other, Mildred wondered if they might possibly be lovers.

Looking at the rest of the company about the table, she saw the couple she had witnessed earlier, and immediately a warmth recalled itself into her loins. The man seemed to feel her gaze and looked in her direction. He winked. Mildred flushed to the roots of her hair and quickly looked down at her soup.

Good heavens. She supposed she ought not feel chagrinned, but the more outlandish aspects of the château required some acclimating. Despite her discomfort, she found herself more eager than ever to engage in the château's purpose. With a life of married ennui before her, she ought to soak in what Château Follet offered.

"Forgive me for introducing myself," the man to her right said, "though we do dispense with the customary formalities here at Château Follet."

"Indeed? I would not have guessed," Mildred replied.

The man smiled in seeming appreciation. "Charming. I must have your name?"

"Miss, er, Abbey."

"Miss Abbey, a pleasure. I am the Viscount Devon."

"Pleased to meet you, my lord."

"You are new to me. Is this your first time?"

"Yes."

With interest, he turned his body farther toward her. "Then you are in for quite a delight."

Happy to have someone to talk to and hopeful that she would not have to spend the evening in her own company, she gave him her most winning smile. Though barely average in height, Lord Devon was quite attractive with his golden locks and bright blue eyes.

He looked to see who sat to her left. It was a woman of striking beauty. Mildred expected he would attempt to make the acquaintance of the woman beside her, but he returned his gaze to her.

"Are you here with someone?" he asked.

"No, I am alone."

"As am I."

The palpitation of her heart quickened. Could this debonair man—a Viscount, if he gave his name truthfully—possibly be interested in her?

Just then, she thought she heard a familiar baritone come from the doors behind her. A mouse coming face to face with a hawk could not have felt more ill.

"Marguerite, your pardon for my late arrival. I am most sorry," the gentleman said.

"La, Andre! You are *not* sorry for being tardy."

"I *am* sorry I was thrown from my horse, which was the cause of my delay."

Mildred did not hear Madame Follet's response. The blood had drained from her.

It could not be. It could not be!

She wanted to turn and look to confirm her fears, but she could not risk revealing herself.

"Miss Abbey, are you well?" Devon asked. "Forgive me, but you look pale of a sudden."

As she faced Devon, she discerned that the man

she suspected to be Alastair stood near the other end of the table, where Madame sat.

"The soup does not agree with me, I think," she whispered.

"But you have hardly touched it."

"I was unsure if you would come," Madame said, "but I have saved you a seat for dinner."

From the corner of her eye, she saw the man rounding the table. She recognized the build, the height, the jet-black hair. Dear heavens, it was Alastair!

In a panic, she bent down behind the table as if she had dropped something.

"Miss Abbey?" Devon inquired, bending down as well.

"I think one of my earrings fell," she said, pretending to look about the floor.

"They are both of them in your ears."

She blinked several times, her mind in a whir. "Oh, well, thank you."

Realizing she could not spend the dinner beneath the table, she sat back up, holding her napkin before her face and keeping herself angled toward her end of the table. Her heart raced. What was she to do? She could not keep her napkin at her face the entire dinner. This was dreadful! She had to find a way to leave.

"I forgot my—my—something—in my chambers," she murmured as she rose.

She would not be able to excuse herself to the hostess but hoped Madame Follet would forgive her later. Alastair sat across the table near the other end. If she turned to her right and went through the set of doors nearest to her, he would not glimpse her face.

Holding the napkin in front of her still, she made for the egress—and walked straight into a maid carrying a tureen of gravy. The contents splashed down the front of Mildred's gown.

"Oh, miss, I'm terribly sorry!" the maid cried.

"Miss Abbey!" Lord Devon cried, coming to her aid.

One of the other gentlemen had approached to help with picking up the tureen.

"I'm quite all right," Mildred mumbled, conscious that half the table had risen to look her way. She reached down for the napkin she had dropped.

Lord Devon took her elbow. "Are you certain—"

"Yes, yes, I am fine," she assured him before stepping into a puddle of gravy in her haste to flee.

Once outside the dining hall, she hurried down the corridor, but her legs had begun to shake with violence. She slipped into an empty but lighted parlor. Closing the door behind her, she leaned against it and sank to the floor.

It was Alastair. She knew his voice, and Madame had called him by name. She was not at all surprised that he would be known to Madame, but how was it he should be here the very same evening as her? And what was she to do now that he was?

Chapter Five

THE ENTICING TEMPTRESS SITTING BESIDE him at the table batted her long lashes and gave him a demure smile. She had shiny crimson curls, and as Alastair had never bedded a redhead before, he was intrigued. Her name was Miss Annabelle Hollingsworth.

But a commotion at the other end of the table drew his attention. He glimpsed a dark-haired woman with gravy down the front of her gown. Her full form looked familiar, as did her gown. At her side was the Viscount Devon, of whom he was not fond, but she resisted the man's aid and hurried from him. She reached down to retrieve a napkin, which she oddly held to her face instead of using it to wipe her dress.

Her right hand tugged at her pearls as she spoke to Lord Devon…

It could not be.

Alastair rose to his feet to take a better look, but she had hurried away. He turned to Marguerite. "Who was that?"

"A new guest," Madame replied. "She arrived here but a few hours ago. You will have the chance to meet her after dinner when we have the pairing."

But an odd ache shot through his legs. He had the sensation whenever a situation was not right. He would have to assure himself that the woman was not whom he thought. He excused himself and proceeded after the woman. In the corridor, however, he saw no signs of her. Likely, she had returned to her chambers to cleanse her gown. He would have to make further inquiries of Marguerite.

Then he noticed the spots of gravy upon the floor. Following the trail, he found it stopped at the closed doors of a parlor. He heard a rustle from inside and opened the doors. Scanning the room, he saw no one, but he was certain he had heard movement. The windows were closed, so the sound had come from inside the room.

He almost dared not utter the name, for fear that doing so might bring about the reality he dreaded. Nevertheless, he tried it.

"Millie."

Silence.

Hoping he was wrong but determined not to rest till he had set his concerns at ease, he walked about the room. He stepped around a sofa and discovered a female form, curled like a mouse upon the floor, hiding behind the furniture, her derriere propped high up in the air.

"Millie!"

She started and scrambled around. She rose slowly, keeping her gaze averted.

"What the devil do you do here?" he demanded, astounded.

"I—I was looking for my, er—"

"Not here in the room. *Here.* The château."

"Oh, well…" She had an inspiration and met his gaze. "What do *you* do here?"

"I will have none of your impudence, my girl. Why are you here?"

Her chin tilted up as she attempted as much dignity as she could while covered in gravy. "That is no affair of yours."

He drew in a sharp breath. "How is it not my affair?"

"Because it is not! And since when do you concern yourself with others?"

A muscle rippled along his jaw. He supposed it did not matter what her answer might be. He would have to see to her departure. The Château Follet was no place for her. He had made a promise to his aunt, and though he had thought he might fulfill her wish by taking a mild interest in one of his young nephews, she would be devastated if he did not rescue his cousin, whom he knew Katherine to be partial to.

"How did you come here?" he asked. "Are you here with someone?"

"I am here alone," she said. "Now if you would kindly step aside, I should like to return to my chambers and divest myself of this gravy."

But he blocked her path. "That does not suffice. You say you are here alone, but how did you arrive?"

"By horse and carriage."

He was torn between appreciating her ready

retort and a desire to wring her neck. This was not the Millie he knew. Why was she behaving with such insolence?

He narrowed his eyes. "Your parents would not permit their only daughter to travel alone. Who brought you here?"

There was a stubborn set to her jaw, and it was clear she concealed something. His mind raced through the possibilities. He had not noticed Haversham's presence and doubted the man was the sort of fellow Marguerite would invite to her château. Alastair considered Millie's set of friends, but as much as they liked to flirt with danger, they were too naïve. Who else among Millie's acquaintances could possibly...

No. It could not be. Yet who else would know of Château Follet?

He pressed his lips together. "Katherine."

Millie's face fell.

"Did you think me so dull-witted that I would not guess? Where is she?" he asked.

"She left to stay with a friend and will return on the morrow."

He suppressed an oath. Setting aside his disbelief that his aunt would do such a thing as introduce Millie to the Château Debauchery, he fixed his mind to how he was going to take Millie away. He had not come by carriage but by horseback. He would have to borrow Marguerite's carriage. He silently cursed. He had been looking forward to his stay at the château for some time, and instead of spending his nights with the beautiful redhead who had caught his interest, he would be chaperoning his gravy-adorned cousin away.

"We start the festivities *after* dinner. How naughty of you two to depart the dinner table—and without a by-your-leave."

They both turned to see Marguerite at the threshold. Looking radiant in a gown that appeared to cling to her slim frame, she sauntered toward them.

Millie flushed and lowered her eyes. "Forgive the impoliteness, Madame Follet."

"Marguerite, I have need of your carriage," he said.

The hostess raised her perfectly arched brows. "My carriage? You are not leaving?"

"I fear we must."

"'We?'"

"Miss Abbott and I. Tonight."

Millie looked up. "I made no mention of leaving."

He turned to her. "You are certainly not staying."

"Lady Katherine expects to fetch me from here tomorrow."

"I will sort the matter out with my aunt when I see her."

He still could not believe what Katherine had done. What was she thinking?

"*Mon dieu*," Marguerite exclaimed. "I do not understand. Why must anyone leave? You are both of you but arrived."

He spoke before Millie could respond. "This is no place for a respectable young woman—your pardon, Marguerite—and one who is betrothed!"

Marguerite looked at Millie, whose countenance crumbled. "It is true," she admitted. "I own it is most unseemly—"

"La, my dear! Betrothed, married, or widowed, it matters not," Marguerite said cheerfully. She turned back to him. "I am surprised *you*, of all people, care."

"Miss Abbott is my cousin!" he replied.

"Ah, now I understand. You do not wish a scandal in the d'Aubigne family."

"She is not a d'Aubigne, and I don't bl—care much about scandals."

Millie interjected, "Especially as you have committed more than your fair share of them."

He looked sharply to her before returning to Marguerite. "She will ruin herself if she stays here. No dowry in the world could save her then. Even that Haversham will not have her, I vow."

"And I should not despair at such an outcome," Millie murmured.

He looked once more to her. This was not the Millie Abbott he knew, and he had deemed himself an accurate judge of character.

Marguerite glanced between them. "But how kind of you, Andre, to care so much for the reputation of your cousin. I would not have thought you capable of such tenderness."

He was very near to uttering an oath before two members of the gentle sex. Marguerite had never vexed him before, but he did not like that his consternation seemed to amuse her.

"Your carriage, if you please, Marguerite," he said.

"I have no wish to leave," Millie objected.

"She has no wish to leave," Marguerite echoed.

"It doesn't matter. I am taking her to safety," he

responded, ignoring Millie's indignant gasp. "It is not that I do not esteem you, Marguerite, but you are more inclined to trust than not. And I do not trust all your guests. Especially the Viscount Devon."

"He seemed a most agreeable man to me," Millie said.

His friend and frequent guest of the château, the Baron Rockwell, had warned of Lord Devon. The Viscount had a keen though subtly expressed interest in virgins.

"The more a man charms you, the less you can trust him," he told Millie.

"I suppose you would know a rogue better than anyone."

He blinked, taken aback once more. Was she acting this way because she was cross at him for not intervening in her engagement?

"I take it you must be *close* cousins," Marguerite said, "for you quarrel as easily as an old married couple."

Millie appeared chastened. "Forgive me, Madame Follet. I fear I have given you a poor sampling of my manners. Your pardon as well, cousin. I should be flattered that you wish to preserve my honor. I ought not have responded as I did to your highhandedness. Perhaps it is best I depart."

At last Millie had come to her senses, he thought.

But Marguerite objected. "No, no! I will not see it happen. You, my dear, will change your attire. I will send Bhadra to assist you. You, Andre, will return to the dining room and finish your dinner. It is settled. The both of you will enjoy your time here as you had initially intended."

"Settled?" he echoed. "Nothing is settled."

"It is. Your aunt entrusted Miss Abbott to me with the expectation that she will have a marvelous time, and I will see it done."

She took Millie by the arm and began to guide her toward the door.

"Do you mean to say you are refusing my request for the use of your carriage?"

"*C'est cela.*"

He stopped her. "Marguerite, pray be reasonable. You do Miss Abbott no favors by permitting her to stay."

"Andre, she is *my* guest, not yours. Your aunt—"

"Katherine is far too enamored with this place and in want of discretion."

Marguerite arched her slender brows. "Andre, this is most unlike you. And because we are good friends, I will dare to say that I find your position rather selfish."

She astounded him. She deemed him selfish when he was willing to sacrifice his long-awaited weekend at the château to protect his cousin?

His look of vexation did not daunt Marguerite. She continued, "*Oui.* You have partaken readily of the pleasures here but would deny the opportunity to another?"

He tried a different approach. "I ask you, as a friend, I beg of you to see the soundness of my actions."

"Your aunt is my friend as well, and I am loath to disappoint her."

They had all lost reason, he decided. All three women. Women he had hitherto thought sensible—especially Millie.

"I do not mean to disparage you or the château, Marguerite," he said, unrelenting, "but it is not worth the risk for Miss Abbott."

"Sir, you presume too much on my behalf," Millie said.

Marguerite put a gentle hand upon his arm. "It is *trés* amusing to see you fret in the manner of an old woman, but I assure you that all will be well."

His vexation trapped all words. If she were not the hostess, he would have a few choice words for her.

Marguerite turned to escort Millie from the room, but he stopped them. Addressing Millie, he said, "Do not be a fool. I am willing to chaperone you home, but I may not be so generously inclined later."

She straightened. "I thank you for your kind offer, Alastair, but it is not necessary."

His nostrils flared. The chit should be grateful for his selfless gesture!

"Stop such idiocy, Millie. You do not fully comprehend what transpires here."

"I have been well informed by both your aunt and Madame Follet."

"And the wiser course would be for you to reconsider!"

"How is it the wiser course for me but not for you?" she cried.

"Are you truly asking such a daft question? I had thought you more sensible than that."

She flushed with indignation. "I intended to draw attention to your *hypocrisy* with my question."

"It is not my hypocrisy but that of society's. The

consequences fall much more harshly upon the female sex."

"But here at Château Follet, the sexes are equal," declared Marguerite. "It is a quality you appreciate, *mon chéri*, and benefit from."

"But how will Millie benefit?"

"In the same manner you do, but of course."

"That is different."

"How?"

Why were these women asking such ridiculous question? Did they truly require him to state the obvious?

"Certain ruin awaits her if she is discovered."

"That has yet to happen with a guest."

"She won't like it here."

Millie breathed in sharply. "Surely that is for me to determine."

"I assure you this is no place for you. My dear aunt has not been here in some time and forgets the nature of the acts here would appall you."

"I am not easily frightened or appalled."

"Millie, don't be a dolt."

"I object to your condescension, sir!"

"It is for your own good. You know no one here. What man do you expect will pair with you?"

He saw her eyes widen and regretted the harshness of his words, but it was warranted if he was to talk sense into her.

She looked ready to attack him or cry, possibly both. "You think no one will desire me?"

"That is not what I said."

"It is what you meant!"

He fumed because her accusation was not entirely

untrue. "The men here—their expectations are different."

Her bottom lip quivered. "If I am not selected, then I will take pleasure in watching others."

Her response stunned him into silence.

"Andre, I protest," Marguerite intervened. "Miss Abbott has a right to be here as much as you do, and I dare say, if you do not leave her be, I shall have to ask you to leave."

Astonished, he allowed Marguerite to usher Millie out the room. He released the oath he had been withholding. He was tempted to take the Follet carriage, with or without consent. He cursed again. Without a carriage, he could not transport Millie from the château. He could put her on his horse, but their progress would be slow, if not treacherous at night. It was no way for a lady to travel.

He would simply have to convince Marguerite or Millie that it was wrong for her to stay.

Good God, what was Katherine thinking letting Millie stay at the Château Follet? Alone. And how had Millie consented to such a thing? Did she realize what transpired here? Perhaps if she did, she would more readily depart with him.

He had always known Millie to be a sensible young woman. She was not frivolous, did not play the sort of games in which others of her sex engaged, and spoke with refreshing candor and maturity. For her to risk her honor in such a fashion was unlike her. If she were discovered, she would be ruined. Her family would be ruined.

Damnation. He ought not care. If she chose to be reckless and foolish, it ought to be none of his affair. Birthday wishes be damned. He had come to enjoy himself, to indulge in wicked carnality. As the Marquess of Alastair, he could afford to do as he pleased. Millie had not that luxury.

Chapter Six

SEATED AT THE VANITY IN only her shift and
stays, Mildred did not know whether to laugh
or cry. She must have looked a ridiculous sight to
Alastair with her gravy-soaked dress. After all that
effort to escape the dining hall, he had found her,
on hands and knees, hiding behind a sofa. How
sadly undignified! She shook her head. The whim-
sical hand of Fate could not have contrived a more
aggravating, unsettling coincidence. Yet, despite the
disconcerting appearance of her cousin, she would
rather see her time at the château through. It was
the opportunity of a lifetime, to indulge her most
wanton cravings, to allow those urges the light of
day before they were condemned to darkness for
the remainder of time.

But could such a thing come to pass now that
Alastair was here?

His overbearing manner had riled her, yet she
regretted having been so impertinent with him.
His intentions were honorable. Nevertheless, she
could not help but deem him hypocritical. He,

of all people, should applaud a woman coming to Château Follet. That she should be his cousin ought have no bearing on the matter.

She put her head in her hands. What an impression she must have made to the guests at the dinner table! Especially to Lord Devon. He must think her a blundering idiot. What if no one wished to partner with her? How embarrassed would she be to have that happen in front of Alastair? Oh, this was turning into quite a mess! Perhaps she should leave the château with him.

But if she should be fated to become Mrs. Haversham, this was her last chance to know the pleasures of the flesh, to understand that look of rapture upon Lady Katherine's countenance when she recalled her past at Château Follet. Lady Katherine had facilitated a rare and precious occasion and would be disappointed if such a gift were not made use of. Not seeing her time through here would disappoint Lady Katherine.

As Bhadra dressed her, Mildred reasoned that Alastair would soon forget her in favor of other company, such as the beauty who had sat beside him at the table. His roguish nature would prevail, and he would tend to his own interests. He could commend himself for making an attempt at propriety, but what more could he do? He would not wish to oppose Madame Follet.

Mollified, Mildred turned her thoughts to Lord Devon. Did she dare hope that he would choose her for a partner? She marveled that he seemed to have taken an interest in her, but would his attentions last beyond dinner, especially after he had had the chance to converse with other, lovelier women?

Mildred studied herself in the mirror. She was not striking, but neither was she homely. And she possessed other qualities that must improve her presence, even if her countenance and figure were of middling beauty.

What was it that Alastair had said? That no man would pair with her? In the past, his bluntness rarely ruffled her, but this one hurt. It was her own worst fear made verbal. And while it was a good possibility that no man would take an interest in her beyond making polite conversation at the dinner table, Alastair need not have been so cruel.

Upset that her thoughts had turned once again to her cousin, Mildred started pacing before Bhadra had finished fixing her coiffure.

Lady Katherine had seemed confident that she would find a partner. Perhaps her ladyship had made an arrangement with Madame Follet? But what if she had not?

Mildred reviewed herself in the looking glass. Perhaps if she applied a little more rouge, her appearance would be improved enough to interest the likes of Lord Devon?

No, she needed more than rouge. She needed a lovelier gown, but she had soiled her best dress.

Realizing she was thirsty gave her an idea. She would dampen her gown. The women at the French courts had started such a practice. No man could fail to take notice.

"Remove all but one of the petticoats," she told Bhadra, hardly believing what she was about to do. She wondered what her cousin would think, then reminded herself it mattered not. She did not require his approval, nor would he wish to be bothered for it. His vehemence had surprised her.

"Pay him no heed," she told herself, then told Bhadra of her wishes.

She shivered after water had been applied to the whole of the gown. It was not the most comfortable of sensations, but the effect was provocative, even upon an imperfect form.

"You look lovely, miss," Bhadra said.

"Thank you."

Mildred drew in a fortifying breath, though her nerves, dancing erratically within her, could not be easily calmed. When she felt she had enough command of herself, she headed back down to the dining hall.

Chapter Seven

WITH ANOTHER CURSE, ANDRE MADE his way back to the dining hall, where he took his place once more beside the redhead. She seemed pleased at his return and gave him her whole attention. He attempted to reciprocate, but as her conversation was not the cleverest—she confined herself to marveling at the repast, commenting upon the château decor, and other subjects he found rather tedious—he tried to appreciate her other qualities. She had a slender form, a complexion of alabaster that required no powder, and a lovely cleavage about her lace-trimmed décolletage.

But his attention kept wandering to the other end of the table, where Millie had previously sat next to Lord Devon.

"You say you prefer the town over country?"

Andre turned to Miss Hollingsworth. "Your pardon?"

"The town," she said. "I take it you prefer the many forms of amusement available in London: theaters, clubs, or gaming halls."

He glanced once more toward the other end of the table. Millie had not returned yet.

"Though I suspect, for men, the countryside also holds much appeal in the way of hunting and fishing. We women are less fortunate. We must prefer the town for its superior offerings of entertainment and shopping, yet the streets can be so dirty and the air so polluted. If you were of the gentle sex, would you say London's benefits outweigh its objections?"

Finding her question far too inane, he made no reply.

At that moment, Marguerite returned. He was glad to see that Millie still had not. Perhaps his cousin had come to her senses after all. She could remain in her room the rest of the night till Katherine returned to retrieve her in the morning.

"Surely you must have a preference?" Miss Hollingsworth persisted.

"I should prefer the Château Follet," he answered, hoping to conclude this particular *tête-à-tête* and reminding himself that soon it would not matter that he found her dialogue dull. All that mattered was how lovely she would look sans clothing.

"Above all," he added with a subtle smile.

She flushed, and her brows rose with interest. "I, too, am partial to Château Follet above all other places."

Now *his* brows rose with interest. He had hoped to meet a woman so inclined.

"Have you been here before?"

"Twice. And you?"

"More than twice."

"Then you must be quite *experienced*."

Desire glimmered in her eyes, causing warmth to rise through his loins.

"Ah, Miss Abbey!" he heard Lord Devon remark.

Turning, Andre saw his cousin returned to the dining hall—and nearly fell from his chair.

What the devil had she done to her gown?

The fabric clung to her curves, outlining the swell of her hips and adhering to her thighs. She had wet the dress in the fashion of French harlots. Every eye was ogling her—especially those of Devon, who sprang to his feet to pull a chair for her. Millie smiled and thanked him.

Andre felt his jaw tighten. He looked at Marguerite, but she was busy chatting with her other guests. He looked back toward Millie, who conversed with Devon with an air of ease. Devon was leaning far too closely toward her.

"I had hoped to meet a man of experience upon my trip here."

Andre turned to Miss Hollingsworth. What the devil had she said?

"How long do you stay?"

"Three nights," he replied before glancing once more toward Millie and Devon.

Would Devon truly choose to pair with Millie for the evening? There were plenty of women to choose from, and who might happily receive the company of Lord Devon. The son of an earl, Devon had breeding, a charming smile, and the most stylish clothing that Saville Row had to offer. He could have his pick of women, most of whom were more attractive than Millie, but he seemed intent upon her. Rockwell had said the man could sniff out a virgin a league away.

Andre started, for something touched his knee. It was Miss Hollingsworth. She was cutting the quail upon her plate, but a small smile hovered over her lips. He should be much encouraged by this, but his first thought was whether or not Devon had his knee similarly pressed to Millie's beneath the table.

It ought to be no concern of his, Alastair reminded himself. Millie had decried his interference. He had had no hand in this foolishness Katherine and Millie engaged in. He was not responsible for his cousin's virtue.

It was too much the coincidence. Katherine knew of his plans to be at Château Follet, had quaintly requested that he take someone into his concerns, and, lo and behold, here was his cousin. Was it a test to see if he would make good on the birthday present?

He was not afraid to disappoint his aunt, especially if he was being set up. But what of Millie? She had seemed genuinely horrified to see him. She was far too good for Devon. What if the cad should hurt her? She would surely learn her lesson then and think twice of disregarding her cousin's counsel in the future.

If the worst should come to pass, she and Katherine had no one to blame but themselves.

Chapter Eight

LORD DEVON'S LOOK OF APPRECIATION as he eyed her over from head to toe was all Mildred required to shore her resolve to see her night through at Château Follet, regardless of her cousin's presence.

During the remainder of dinner, she had caught the solemn stare of Alastair more than once and determined that she would stop looking his way. If she were to enjoy herself, she had to pay him no heed. He would surely forget her soon enough, especially as that scarlet beauty beside him clearly took an interest in him, as most women were wont to do.

"You have not touched your pudding," Devon remarked.

"In truth, I am too nervous to eat very much," she answered, though she could not recall the last time she had passed on dessert.

"Ah, that is to be expected your first time here," he said with reassurance.

She returned a grateful smile.

"Perhaps another glass of port will ease the nerves?" he offered, waving at one of the footmen.

Mildred felt the gaze of her cousin upon her but resisted looking at him. She hesitated at a second glass, for she had already consumed a full glass of wine and was not accustomed to partaking of more, but Devon was already instructing the footman to refill her glass.

Devon held up his own glass. "To an unforgettable first time."

She clinked her glass to his before putting it to her lips. Perhaps the glass of port was precisely what she needed. She was surprised at her present disquiet, especially after she had so firmly declared her intention of staying to Alastair.

She finished the glass of port, and from Devon's look of surprise, she must have done so rather quickly.

"The port is far better than the pudding," Devon acknowledged.

Blushing, she replied, "Yes, it is a very fine port."

When Devon made to gesture again for the port, she stayed him, placing a hand upon his arm. "No, no. I will not be seen as a glutton, particularly upon my first visit."

"Madame Follet would welcome your gluttony and be happy to have the offerings of her cellar so enjoyed."

She chanced to look Alastair's way and found him staring in her direction. *Blast it.* She would have thought him lost in the brilliant, thickly lashed eyes of the redhead by now. Realizing her hand still rested upon Devon, she quickly withdrew and straightened in her chair. Devon looked to where she had gazed.

"Do you know that man?" Devon asked.

She waved a dismissive hand. "Hardly."

"It seemed he followed you when you left the table."

Though she had no appetite for food, she decided to take a large spoonful of pudding. "He felt obliged, as my cousin, to see that I was well."

Devon's brows shot up. "Your cousin?"

Having no desire to talk of Alastair, she replied quickly, "By marriage. And we are scarcely in the same company."

"How coincidental that you should both be here then."

"Yes, it was completely unexpected." *And unwanted.*

Devon looked down the table toward Alastair.

"Perhaps I will have another glass of port," she declared to draw his attention.

She accomplished her goal, for he seemed quite happy to supply her with more wine. She did not consume the third glass with quite the same thirst, for she could start to feel the effects from the first two glasses of wine, the chief benefit of which was that she ceased to mind Alastair and fixed upon Devon's increasing charms.

After dinner, everyone retired to an assembly room adorned with paintings, replicas of works such as *The Nude Maja* by Francisco de Goya y Lucientes, and *Venus of Urbino* by Titian. More wine was served by maids and footmen, scantily dressed in the costuming of ancient Egyptians. Millie tried unsuccessfully not to stare at the abundant amount of flesh revealed, wondering if she would ever have enough nerve to parade in front of others with her midsection and the entire lengths of her arms bared. Or, if she were of the other sex, to expose the whole of the chest. She had always liked that part of a man. It was so very different from that of her sex. The width, the taut ridges, were as pleasing to her eye as anything.

The wine having increased her bravado, she found herself commenting to Devon, "Do they not feel chilled?"

"They are accustomed to their state of dress," he answered.

Mildred realized she felt quite warm despite the dampness of her gown. She also felt light in the head and a little unsteady.

"Would you care for a seat, Miss Abbey?" Devon inquired.

How attentive of him, she thought to herself, pleased that he had not yet left her side. She greatly hoped that he would choose her.

"How are the couples selected?" she asked after sitting down on a settee.

Devon sat beside her. "Well, those that did not arrive with someone may choose from the unattached. At present, we are to circulate and acquaint ourselves with each other and, hopefully, find someone with whom we should like to pair."

"Ah, well, you are kind to keep me company, but do not let me stay you from befriending the others here."

"In truth, I have no interest in seeking other company."

She found herself bereft of words and lost in

the shimmer of his beautiful blue eyes. She could hardly believe her fortune! But perhaps he did not mean to imply he preferred her company? Yet, what else could he have intended with those words? Did she dare press for a supporting statement? How she wished she had not partaken of so much wine that she could think more clearly!

"Miss Abbey, may I have a word?"

She looked up to see Alastair standing before them with his hand outstretched, and she was not so inebriated that she could not know from the firm set of his jaw that she was better off *not* taking his hand.

Sensing her hesitation, Devon rose. "Good sir, I do not think I have the pleasure of your acquaintance? I am the Viscount Devon, my father the Earl of—"

"And I am Alastair," her cousin replied, staring coolly at Devon.

Devon bowed. "A pleasure. Is this your first visit to Follett?"

"No, and if you will pardon my intrusion, I mean to have a word with Miss Abbey."

Mildred wanted to refuse, but the tone in his voice suggested that it was perhaps unwise to do so. She turned to the frowning viscount and could see that he wished to object, but his sex was not immune to the command that Alastair exuded.

"I shan't be long," she assured Devon before rising and accepting her cousin's arm.

She allowed herself to be led to the other end of the room and braced herself for battle.

"Have you lost all discretion?" he asked when they had put some distance between them and the other guests.

She would have pulled her arm from him, but he kept it.

"If you mean to scold me," she replied, "I would spare your breath and time for a more worthy pursuit."

He pressed his lips into a line. "Lord Devon is not to be trusted."

"Yes, you had warned me of his charms."

"A sinister disturbance lurks behind his pretty manners."

"You are well acquainted with him then?"

"It is not necessary for me to be well acquainted with him."

"Then you have no specifics, and no evidence to criticize a man you barely know."

"I require none. I am inclined to dislike him."

They both looked back toward Devon, who was now in conversation with the beautiful redhead.

"You are inclined to dislike *everyone*," Mildred responded with some exasperation, for she wanted to return to Lord Devon and did not like how tightly her arm was trapped against Alastair.

"You are ready to give your trust to a man you just met?"

"I understand that Madame Follet does not extend her invitations to merely anyone."

"She is not immune from making mistakes."

"I am willing to take that chance."

His countenance darkened. "You are willing, then, to award a man who may prove to be a cad your maidenhead? Once given, it cannot be recalled."

She flushed and tried once more to disengage her

arm. When the effort proved fruitless, she stared him square in the eyes and said, "That honor has already been bestowed on another!"

His eyes widened in surprise, and she felt a small triumph in being able to astonish the man. A maid presented them with her tray of wine glasses, and Mildred reached for one.

"You have had enough of that," Alastair growled. To the maid, he said, "A glass of water or lemonade for the mademoiselle."

After the maid had left, he turned back to Mildred. The shock had not left him.

"You are no longer a virgin?" he asked.

"You see, I am more suited to Château Follet than you think."

"But who—with whom—?"

"That is none of your affair."

"I can make it my affair."

"I do not presume to ask the names of the women you have deflowered."

His nostrils flared. "I do not defl—"

"Perhaps you could make it known to Haversham that I am no longer in possession of my honor? For certain he will not wish to marry me then."

"That is the wine talking. When you have come to your senses, you will see what a preposterous notion that would be. I know you would not shame your family in such a way. Despite what Katherine or Marguerite might have said to you, coming to Château Follet carries great risk for you. And you have worsened it by befriending a suspect man and allowing him to intoxicate you!"

"He did not intoxicate me! I drank the port of my own free will."

"Which he encouraged and supplied for you."

Alastair had paid more attention to her during the dinner than she would have thought. It was all very trying and slightly incomprehensible, which made her mind swim. With auspicious timing, the maid returned with a glass of lemonade, which Alastair took and presented to Mildred.

"Drink it," he commanded.

Hoping that doing so would bring about an earlier conclusion to their dialogue, she did as he bid.

"Who was it?" he asked after she had finished half the beverage.

"Who was what?" she returned.

He looked about, then drew her from the room, closing the doors behind them. "Who deflowered you?"

"I said it was none of your affair. It serves you no purpose to know."

"If I were your father or your brother, I would call the rogue out."

"But you are neither."

"Thank God!" they said in unison.

Alastair shook his head and she returned to drinking her lemonade. It did seem to clear the fogginess of her thoughts.

"Nevertheless," he said, "you are connected to the d'Aubigne family now."

"And since when do you trouble yourself with regard to anyone?"

"Since… You think me that heartless?"

She paused. She did not think him so wholly uncaring. If she had, she would never have bothered with speaking to him. But it was best not to think better of him at present. "I thought you prided yourself on your indifference to others?"

"I do."

"Then why waste your breath on me?"

"Because there is one person I *do* care for: my aunt. And she concerns herself greatly with you."

"Ah, you are doing her a favor."

"I am."

"But she wishes me here, wishes me to partake of what Château Follet offers. Are you not doing her a disservice by attempting to thwart her plans?"

"Her wishes are misguided. She will see that soon enough."

"Or she will find you insufferably arrogant."

He grinned. "She has already accepted and made peace with my conceit."

Mildred sighed. The man had an answer for everything! She thought of Devon and the redhead. "Will you not tend to your scarlet beauty before she is charmed by the Viscount?"

He paused before saying, "She will have to wait."

"And why is that? I think our *tête-à-tête* has lasted long enough, and I had said to Lord Devon—"

"Devon and Miss Hollingsworth can keep each other company tonight."

Taken aback, she asked, "I thought you took an interest in the redhead?"

"I did, but I informed Marguerite that for tonight, I am choosing to claim *you*."

Chapter Nine

MILLIE STARED AT HIM WITH her mouth agape. The port had slowed her wits but had yet to make her dumb.

"What an abominable jest!" she huffed when she had come to.

She turned toward the doors, but Alastair stayed her. "I am not the bantering sort, am I, Millie?"

"And you picked a pretty time to start with such nonsense!"

She pulled on the door, but he put his arm to it to keep it shut. She glared at him.

"Let me pass," she demanded. "They might have started the pairing."

"They likely have, but you shall not be returning."

Her lower lip fell once more, and her eyes widened. "You mean to keep me away—"

"From that Devon fellow. Most assuredly."

"What of Miss Hollingsworth? Surely you do not prefer my company over hers?"

"It matters not. You are staying with me tonight

till Katherine returns for you in the morning."

Now her lower lip trembled. "How dare you, sir! You are not my keeper, my father, nor a brother."

"All true but of no consequence to me."

He could see her thoughts swirling chaotically through her head.

"You've no right!"

"It disturbs me little if you wish to think me a tyrant."

"But I did not choose to be with you!"

"It only matters that *I* chose *you*."

"I protest! Madame Follet will hear me."

"Marguerite has approved our match."

"That can't be true! I will speak with her—"

"Only upon my permission."

She stared at him as if he were daft and attempted to yank the door open.

"This is madness, Alastair! You are ruining the night for both of us."

"For which you will thank me when you have returned to your senses."

She looked ready to scream at him. He had never seen his cousin lose her composure before and was mildly interested by the prospect, for the culpability of the night's ruin must be traced to her for coming to the château in the first place.

"You will forfeit the company of that ravenous beauty to mind me?" she tried.

"Never say I never did anything for you, Millie."

Now she looked ready to pommel him. She emitted a frustrated grunt and kicked him in the shin. Surprised, he let his arm slip from the door. She pulled the handle, yanking the door into him, but he recovered and shut it closed.

"Right," he said, scooping her up and throwing her over his shoulder. He headed toward her chambers.

"Alastair!" she yelped. "Put me down! Alastair!"

He resisted her struggles and mounted the stairs. He knew the chambers Marguerite would have given to a newcomer.

Millie tried to right herself upon his shoulder. "Who is the one acting ridiculous? Alastair! Come to your senses!"

She strained against him, trying to wriggle off, but he did not set her down till they were in her chambers.

"I wonder what Lady Katherine would say if she knew of your conduct?" Millie cried. Her coiffure had slipped and now sat askew upon her head. A rosy flush spread across her cheeks, but it was not unbecoming.

"I fully intend to have a word with my aunt about this," he replied. "I will send for Bhadra to pack your belongings, that you may leave as early as possible in the morning. Till then, you are to stay in your chambers."

"I protest this highhandedness!"

"Protest away," he grumbled as he took his leave, closing the door and locking it.

Behind him, he heard the scream she had been withholding.

He blew out his breath and ran a hand through his hair. What a mess. But at least Millie was safe from Devon. For a moment, he considered returning to the assembly room to see if Miss Hollingsworth might, by chance, be still available. But it would not be right to lock Millie in her room for the night whilst he enjoyed himself.

After finding Bhadra and instructing her to prepare a cup of tea and milk, he sought his valet, who was understandably surprised to learn they should prepare to travel in the morning. His valet, a strapping blackamoor, was rather popular at the château and visibly disappointed at their early departure.

Alastair stopped by his own chambers to avail himself of a glass of brandy. He shook his head. This was what was got when he concerned himself in the affairs of others. He did not like that Katherine had forced his hand, but he could not bring himself to completely disregard the woman who had looked over him like a mother. Katherine had said the selection with whom to fulfill her birthday wish was his, but she had chosen for him. His aunt could be quite wily.

He briefly wondered how invested Marguerite was in the collusion. She had readily blessed his selection for the night. Given how she had defended Millie's right to be here, he had expected her hesitation or objection. Instead, she had seemed rather pleased and had made no inquiries at all into whether or not Millie had consented to the match.

What would have happened if he hadn't foiled Katherine's setup? He could easily have minded his own affairs and partaken of the indulgence he had been anticipating the past sennight. If the only risk to Millie was that she might be discovered, he would, perhaps, have accepted the chances. But Devon, too, had forced his hand. The Viscount seemed genuinely interested in Millie.

Alastair supposed he ought not be terribly surprised. Though no beauty, Millie was not unpleasant to the eye. While she had not the elegance of a slender form, she, like the women in a Reuben painting, still held the appeals of her sex. And she was an intelligent creature and far more fearless than he had expected.

And libidinous. Good God, she was not a virgin. He had not suspected *that*. And of all places, she wanted to remain at Château Follet. There was much more to Millie than met the eye. Much more.

"The tea and milk you desired, my lord," Bhadra said from his chamber threshold.

Finishing off his brandy, he gestured for Bhadra to follow him. He would ensure Millie drank the tea and milk while Bhadra prepared the portmanteau so that there would be no delay in departure in the morning. He would then suggest that Millie rest in preparation for the morrow's journey.

But when he and Bhadra entered the chambers, they discovered the room empty.

"What the devil..." he cursed after looking about the room. Then he noticed the balcony doors slightly ajar. He jerked them open and stepped outside.

Chapter Ten

MILDRED NEARLY LOST HER FOOTING as she landed on the adjacent balcony. Perhaps leaping from one balcony to another while one's faculties were a little clouded by wine was not the wisest. But she would not be made a prisoner in her chambers, especially by her cousin, who had no right to interfere in her affairs—well, not since he had declined to intervene in her engagement. She tested the balcony doors and found them locked. She looked to the next nearest balcony. Fortunately, it was not a far jump. She climbed onto the railing and leaped. She stumbled and fell to one knee as she landed. A bruise might come of it, but she was otherwise unharmed. She dusted off her gown and tried the balcony doors. This set was unlocked, and she let herself in.

"Pardon me, monsieur," she gasped when she saw a couple in amorous embrace upon the bed. They were, unsurprisingly, startled to see her.

"I, er, lost my way," Mildred explained as she made for the chamber doors.

"You are more than welcome to watch," the man said.

Mildred felt her face burn. "A gracious invitation, sir, but I must return to the assembly room."

She hustled out of the room and down the hall. She could not recall a more embarrassing scene, though discovering her cousin during dinner was more upsetting. What an insufferable man he was. He had never before shown any interest in her. Why did he choose now to meddle? And how was she going to rid herself of his intrusion?

Hoping that she would not cross his path, she hurried back to the assembly room. She would not be surprised if Lord Devon had forsaken her and chosen another, but she had to find out. She opened the doors to the assembly room, only to find it empty. The pairings must have been completed. Perhaps Lord Devon had gone off with Miss Hollingsworth.

Disappointment welled in her bosom. She had truly thought Lord Devon might choose her for the night. If he had, the château would've surpassed all expectation. She would not have been surprised if she had gone unselected. Thus, the fact that she was alone was something she had been prepared for, but it was not as easy to bear once her hopes had been raised. Now all hope was dashed, thanks to her cousin.

Or perhaps he was right that no one would have chosen her. Perhaps Lord Devon was merely being nice to her. When presented with the chance to be with the likes of Miss Hollingsworth, what man of sense would choose Mildred Abbott?

With a sigh, she sat down on the settee and

wondered what she should do with herself. Should she return to the room she had left a moment ago and accept the man's invitation to watch? Could she be so bold? Why not?

But what if Alastair objected? Well, it was not his place to dictate what she could or could not do. He might think it because he was providing her dowry. Nevertheless, it was not *her* place to be ungrateful.

Regardless, she had not come to the château to twiddle her thumbs. She rose to her feet and looked about. If Alastair found her, he would lock her in her chambers once more, and she had no wish to go to bed just yet. Leaving the assembly room, she made her way down the corridor, away from the stairs that led to her chambers.

She gasped when she passed by a set of double doors that opened to an expansive room full of art. From the threshold, she marveled at the volume of paintings, ceramics, tapestries, castings, sculptures and lithograph. All with themes and subjects were intended to titillate. Entering further, Mildred first examined the more benign oi paintings of a woman naked but for a sheet draped over her legs, another of a woman bathing in a pond, and the third of a naked man stretched across the grass in a pastoral setting. Mildred moved onto the tapestries on the next wall. The tapestries did not show the human form in as realistic detail as the oil paintings, but the nature of the subjects were much more naughty as they depicted various men and women, some with clothing, some without, in obvious congress. Turning about, she beheld a collection of Greek pottery. Here the wantonness deepened. One plate appeared to show two women caressing one another. The vase beside the plate showed two men in similar passions.

"Oh, my," Mildred said when her gaze went beyond the pottery to a sculpture of a naked man, his form as chiseled as that of Michelangelo's David, with one notable difference: the male appendage stood straight and tall. Approaching the sculpture, she examined the erection. The stableboy she had tumbled had not possessed a member half the size of the one upon the statue Was the latter an exaggeration or could a man possibly have an erection of such thickness and length?

A warmth had begun stirring in the lower parts of her body, and the heat and wonder only grew as she observed more wickedness in a set of lithographs. In one, the couple was dressed in the garments of the previous century, but the voluminous skirts did not hamper the woman's ability to display her most private parts. The man, in full dress, also displayed his wares; it pointed at moss loss of hair between her thighs. In the second lithograph, the man stood. The woman was upon her knees and appeared to be in the act of taking his member into her mouth. Mildred felt her mind reeling. For what purpose would a woman and man engage in such an act? The stableboy had asked her to kiss his "sword," as he had called it. She had done so—quickly—for it had seemed unnatural, uncouth, bawdy... and lascivious.

Unsettled by the conflicting emotions that the art had elicited within her, Mildred took a step back. She bumped into the table behind her. It teetered, and the bronze figurines upon it fell to the rug below. Thankfully, nothing was broken. She picked up the figure of a prone and naked man and the figure of a prone and naked woman. She supposed they must have been lying in congress. She put the male figure upon the table and the woman atop it, but they did not appear to fit properly. She placed the woman below and the man on top. Still the positioning looked awkward. She tried adjusting the figures.

"You have replaced them incorrectly."

Startled, she dropped one of the figures.

Alastair stood at the threshold, his arms crossed, his lips in a frown.

She bent down and struck the back of her head on the underside of the table in her attempt to retrieve the figure. She tried placing the female figure atop the male figure again.

Alastair shook his head.

Squaring her shoulders, she met her cousin's gaze and waited in silence until he strode over, took the female figure, rotated the body and placed it atop the male figure. Now the figures sat atop the table securely and the limbs of both figures did not appear at incongruous angles.

But surely this could not be how th artist intended the figures to fit? For the woman's crotch was upon the man's head, and her face was buried upon his...

Heat colored her cheeks. At that, Alastair said, "We should return to your chambers."

"There is no need for you to make me a prisoner, sir. I have lost what chance I might have

GEORGETTE BROWN

had with Lord Devon, slim though my prospects might have been. You need no longer worry that I might fall into the wrong hands."

She made no mention of the invitation from the couple she had stumbled across.

Alastair took her by the elbow. "I cannot trust you to your own devices. Climbing balconies in the dark—while inebriated—is hardly prudent activity."

She yanked her arm from him. "If you had not put me in so desperate a situation, I never would have considered it."

"All this is *my* doing?"

"I certainly did not ask to be so rudely handled by you. Perhaps if you had granted my request of the dowry, neither one of us would be in such an unsatisfactory situation."

She spoke unfairly, but she was too cross at him to mind.

"You may satisfy yourself that, after tonight, I shall never concern myself with you again."

"Thank God!"

He stared at her, and she wondered at the wisdom of her boldness when she saw a vein at this temple throb.

"Stop behaving like a child, Millie."

He reached once more for her, but she avoided him.

"I am merely exploring the château. What objection could you have to that?"

"I object to what you will encounter. There are sights here that are not for the delicate—"

"Sights such as this?" She gestured to the room. "They do not frighten me. They *intrigue* me."

"Because you have little experience with any of this."

"And that is precisely why I have come to Chateau Follet!"

A muscle rippled along his jaw.

"My constitution is not as slight as you would presume."

"Nevertheless." He started dragging her toward the doors. "There is far more depravity here than you could ever imagine."

"You know not what I have imagined."

He paused to look at her but then continued to pull her toward the exit.

"I protest!" she cried. "If I were Miss Hollingsworth, you would not treat me in such a brutish manner."

"Indeed, and you are not Miss Hollingsworth, as you say."

She resisted his tugging. "You think me a simpleton, naïve and innocent. You insist on this characterization of me, but it is not the truth. I have engaged far more than you know, than I have divulged."

"I doubt that what you have done compares to what occurs here at the château. What you fancy might be curious goings-on here are far more daunting when experienced in the flesh."

She attempted to free her arm from his tight grasp. "But I wish to experience it! All of it!"

"All?"

She looked to the bronze figures upon the table. "Yes, *all*."

" You wish to take a man's member into your mouth?"

"I have tasted of it before."

He stopped. "I don't believe you."

"I most certainly have. You see, there is a side of me you do not know. No one knows save Lady Katherine. She came upon me once with the stablehand. She saw my prurience. Thankfully, she did not condemn me for it. Everyone else sees me as this plain, boring spinster-in-the-making. But there is more to me than meets the eye. It is not a part of me I exalt. Till Lady Katherine had come upon me, I was much ashamed of these wayward desires, but they have strength unto themselves. And this is my last chance to explore them, to better understand them. You know not how relieved I was to think that perhaps I am not such the rare deviant. And now that I am to wed Haversham, I shall never be able to satiate this fiery thirst! This was my last and only chance."

Her bottom lip trembled, and tears seemed to come from nowhere, threatening to spill profusely from her eyes. She looked away, not wanting Alastair to see the glisten in her eyes. It was enough that she had bared her soul to him. Merciful heavens. She had said a great many things to him just now. What precisely had she said?

Silence permeated the air between them as she attempted to contain the trembling that had taken hold of her.

"Then let us proceed with this wish of yours."

She looked at him, perplexed. "Pardon?"

"This last chance of yours. Let us make the most of it."

Chapter Eleven

TO HIS CONSTERNATION, HIS HEART
was not as black and impenetrable as Alastair
would have preferred, and Millie's words had struck
an oddly tender part. He had not discovered the
darker side of his desires in the same manner as
she. He had begun to find congress with the regular
strumpet or opera dancer a trifle uninspiring. After
Katherine had introduced him to Château Follet, a
new realm of indulgence had opened to him.

He knew not what he would have thought of
himself if he had harbored such inclinations before
his introduction to Château Follet. He doubted
he would have been as critical of himself as Millie
was of *herself*, but hers was a superior character.
He had sensed it, and though this new part of her
was a shock to him, he still stood by his initial
assessment of her qualities.

He would never have suspected her capable of a
bold prurience, but her response to this discovery
of herself was quite what he would have expected.
Here was an upstanding young woman who
attempted to live up to the expectation of family
and society. These lustful and naughty proclivities
must have come as quite the horror to her, and

were he a man better skilled with words, he would have assured her there was naught to be ashamed of. But finer speech did not come readily to him.

So he kissed her.

Her lips were soft beneath his. He held the side of her head as he moved over her mouth. At first, perhaps too startled, she did not move. She put a hand to his wrist but did not pull him away. He brushed his lips over hers several times before lifting his head to view her.

Her eyes, glistening with tears and the remnants of the port, were wide. He had never before taken note of the soft brown coloring in her eyes. It was quite a lovely hue. And though the flush across her nose was perhaps not so complimentary, the redness would dissipate when she was done weeping.

He groaned to himself. He was going to regret this. Greatly. But for him to retreat now would deal an unnecessary blow. The night had been difficult enough for her.

"What—what do you mean?" she asked, quivering. Her eyes possessed the same glassy brightness that most of her sex had after a kiss.

"You've a wish to indulge in the offerings of Château Follet, do you not?"

"Y-Yes."

"We are both of us without partners."

She continued to stare at him rather stupidly.

He sighed. "As I do not trust anyone with your honor, I will assume your introduction to Château Follet myself."

She was silent.

"Of course, if you would rather not..." He half

hoped she would balk and force him to rescind his offer, but she did not, and remained in thought.

"As we are cousins," he added.

"Not by blood," she said, lowering her eyes, her hand still upon his wrist.

Hell and damnation. He could not recall a more absurd attempt than what he had just engaged. But Millie might yet come to her senses. The port would wear off…

She looked up at him. "It is a strange offer, but you are both gracious and kind, Alastair."

Her countenance had brightened, and he was pleased to see it. He returned a wry smile. The adjectives of "gracious and kind" had not been applied to him before—not by the intelligent and reasonable. Relief waved over him. She had come to her senses.

"I am sorry your evening was not what you had wished," he said.

"But, thanks to you, it may be salvaged in part." He blinked.

"Did I mistake your offer?" she asked when he said nothing.

"I thought you meant to decline it."

"No! I meant to accept it. Unless…you did not mean what you said?"

"Not at all," he replied gruffly. "I merely thought you had perhaps found it too awkward a proposition."

"It seems *you* find it awkward, my lord." She withdrew her hand from him. "You need not worry, Alastair. I will not compel you. I know I am not the most comely of maids."

A stronger oath went through him. He grabbed

her and crushed her to him. She emitted half a yelp before his mouth descended upon hers, his lips harshly roving over hers. His hand went into her coiffure, yanking her head back by the hair.

"If we are to proceed, I will have none of your impudence," he growled. "You will abide by all that I say. Fail me and the evening shall be at an end."

She nodded.

He shook his head. A goddamn stablehand.

Still hoping that time would fade her intoxication, and hence her fearlessness, he said, "First, let us first finish your survey of the art."

They came to a set of engravings under the title *De omnibus Veneris Schematibus.*

"What are these?" she asked.

He translated the Latin for her. "*The Sixteen Pleasures.* These are recreations. The original edition was destroyed by the Catholic Church."

"Who was the creator of the original?"

"Marcantonio Raimondi, who supposedly based his images upon the paintings of Giuilio Romano."

"And here I thought you had little affinity for anything beyond cards and horseflesh."

"When I was at Oxford, a number of fellows attempted a printing of the engravings along with Aretino's sonnets. Both made quite the round amongst the students till the dean discovered them and threatened expulsion of anyone caught with the scandalous material."

Mildred studied the first engraving, *Paris et Oenone*, depicting the Grecian couple in carnal embrace beneath a tree. Lying with her back against the tree, Oenone had one leg between the legs of Paris and her other wrapped about his hip. The second engraving, *Angelique et Medor*, drew even closer study from Mildred. Set against a woodland background, Medor, naked, lay upon the ground, while Angelique, also naked, attempted to sit atop him, her hand between her legs holding his member to guide it into her.

"Are they from Greek mythology?" Mildred asked, her voice husky.

"They are characters from the Italian epic *Orlando Furioso* by Ludovico Ariosto," Andre answered.

"I do not know it."

"Angelica was an Asian princess at the court of Charlemagne. She fell in love with the Saracen knight Medoro, and eloped with him to China."

"Is this position of theirs comfortable?"

Andre supposed the port lent her courage or she would not possess such ease in asking such a bold question of him.

"You would have to ask them," he deflected. This was not the sort of conversation he had ever imagined having with his cousin.

She wrinkled her nose at his response. "Have *you* ever performed this position?"

He started and began to think twice about evading her questions, lest she make him pay with more audacious queries.

"Have you?" she prompted.

He stared at her. He saw that she intended no impudence for curiosity sparkled in her eyes. He answered, "Yes."

"And was it uncomfortable?"

"Not for me."

"And what of the woman?"

He tugged at his cravat for it grew warm about his neck. "I have heard no complaints before."

She turned to look once more at the engraving, and he was glad to have her probing eyes off him.

"Is it enjoyable?"

Perhaps, if she intended to have a great many questions of this nature, it was not wise to continue their survey of the art.

"Yes," he replied, hoping she would not require elaboration.

"For both parties?"

"Yes."

"How can you be certain of *hers*?"

"I am."

"But how?"

He rubbed his temples. "From her cries of pleasure. In fact, it is quite a desirable position for the woman if her legs possess the stamina."

"Indeed? How so?"

"I have only anecdotal evidence, but I draw my conclusion from the many repeated requests for this position."

She appeared deep in thought, then moved to the third engraving of a satyr and nymph. A mound at the foot of a tree served as a chair for the nymph to sit upon while the satyr prepared to spear his member into her womanhood. To Andre's relief, she asked no questions of this engraving.

"This is not unlike the second," she remarked of the fourth engraving, *Julie Avec Un Athlete*, in which the man was upon hands and feet, but with the body turned upward as if to form a table top with the chest and torso, while the woman straddled him, "but appears much more difficult."

"I have not attempted this position in its exact form," he said hastily.

The fifth engraving made Mildred straighten. "Surely this is not possible? Not a for a sustained period."

He said nothing as he looked upon the engraving, *Hercule et Dejanire*. Hercules stood upright holding Dejanire in his arms, his erection buried inside her.

"You do not contradict me," she noted. Her eyes narrowed. "You have done this position."

Many times, he thought to himself.

"Is this position superior in enjoyment?"

He turned to face her, wanting an end to her queries. "A definitive principle cannot be stated. Your enjoyment will differ from mine and even those of other woman, just as the preference for hues and fashion varies in your sex."

Satisfied, she moved on to the engraving, *Ovide et Corine.*

"I suspect this a more common position," she said of the couple in bed. Corine lay upon the legs spread and Ovide between them.

Upon moving to *Mars et Venus,* she said, "Though I have tried this position as well."

The two gods were locked in nude embrace upon a bed. Mars lay against the pillows with Venus upon her knees, settling atop his tall erection.

"Good God, how many times has the stableboy given you a gown of green?" Andre asked.

She made no reply but laughed at the next engraving. "This I very much doubt would be comfortable for the woman."

In *Bachus et Ariane,* Bachus stood holding Ariane, upside down with her face planted in the pillow upon the ground, by the legs.

"It looks as if he intends to use her as a wheelbarrow!" Mildred said.

"It is one of the more difficult positions to sustain," he admitted as he recalled his first attempt.

"You have tried this one as well? Is there naught you have not attempted?"

Remembering that she had not answered his earlier question, he began, "This stableboy—"

She waved a dismissive hand. "I am done with him. He no longer works for your aunt."

Andre would have to have a word with Katherine about her employment decisions.

"I wish I had your liberty to attain such experiences," she said as she glanced through the rest of the engravings. Most were variations of the first several they had seen.

Her statement prompted him to ponder a society in which women had similar freedoms to men to pursue their passions. As women possessed the same desires as men, and to the same depths, though most would not exhibit the truth of it as readily as his cousin did, there was much sense in removing the shackles that burdened the gentler sex.

"I think *Angelique et Medor* to be my favorite," Mildred pronounced. "I should like to try this position. May we?"

He turned to her with a frown. Though the engravings had provoked a warmth inside him, and though he had begun to see that Mildred was not as plain as he had first thought her, he was not prepared to ravish her.

But then he noticed the unevenness of her breath, her parted lips, and the blush in her cheeks. The primal in him stirred.

Chapter Twelve

HE WAS HESITATING, SHE SAW. Was it because she had not the beauty of Miss Hollingsworth? Did propriety, a quality which, till tonight, she would have doubted to reside in his bosom, stay him? But then, why had he kissed her? The pressure of his lips still lingered. His offer had taken her completely by surprise, and if he had not wanted her to accept, he ought not have kissed her. She understood now why so many of her sex delighted in his presence. They knew what he was capable of.

She had known it, too, but as she knew she would never receive his attention in that way, she had suppressed her acknowledgment of these qualities in Alastair. And because he had many faults that she did not admire, she had chosen not to see his seductive qualities. They might as well have been cousins by blood.

Alastair was right. If she had been in full command of her faculties, if her reservations were not thawed by the port, she would not have allowed this to come to pass. She would not be standing before him in a room full of naughty art, propositioning him.

Alastair narrowed his eyes. "This stableboy. How many times have you lain with him?"

She frowned at the stall. "What does it matter?"

"How many?" he demanded.

"More than once."

His pupils constricted, and a muscle along his jaw rippled.

"But not more than thrice," she added with exasperation.

In disbelief, he exclaimed, "Thrice?"

"The first instance should count not, as the act could not be completed. I think my cries frightened him. His, er, entry hurt more than I thought it would."

Alastair shook his head. "Where is the little bleeder now?"

"Do you suggest that you would have done differently than him? You, who have lifted the skirts of any number of women—how many have you taken into your bed?"

"I have never deprived a woman of her maidenhead."

"The Marquess of Alastair has *scruples*? Dear me, what have you done with my cousin?"

She yelped when he closed the distance between them and gripped her arm. "Take care, Millie, my tolerance of your insolence wears thin."

"I was merely calling out your hypocrisy. Would you truly have hesitated to tumble a willing maiden?"

He released her, perhaps in acknowledgment of

her point.

"I would you did not hesitate now," she said more quietly. The art had provoked a roiling tension in her body, and she wanted release. "Perhaps we could...retire to your bedchamber?"

He stared at her, and she could not make out his expression save that his earlier anger might have dissipated. His pupils had dilated.

"If you had not wanted the boldness you now possess," he replied, "you would not find yourself engaged to Haversham."

She acknowledged this to be true. "As such, I am now in some desperation, and desperation breeds courage."

"Or foolhardiness."

She waved a dismissive hand, impatient to address the longing inside her. "Let us say I am *determined*."

"That you are."

If she were not awash in port and desire, she might have thought her cousin to speak with a dash of admiration.

"We are a long way from my bedchamber," he said, his voice slightly husky.

"Do you intend to retract your offer?" she asked, upset by his delays. "You would not with my father, but perhaps you are less inclined to integrity because I am a woman?"

His hand circled the back of her neck, drawing her in close. She gasped at the tightness of his grip. Perhaps her desperation did engender foolishness. She had already tried his patience. Why was she choosing to provoke him further? Poking a sleeping tiger with a stick might be a wiser act.

"I think what you truly desire is a sound spanking," he said near her ear.

A shiver went through her. She swallowed with difficulty before responding, "Did I vex you? I thought you cared not a wit what accusations are thrown at you?"

He released her. A grin seemed to tug at one corner of his lips. She tried not to stare at his mouth and recall how delicious his had felt upon hers.

"Indeed," he declared, crossing his arms. "Let us commence that which you desire. There is no need to waste time retiring to a bedchamber."

She furrowed her brow. *What did he mean?*

"We do not require a bedchamber and have more than we need here."

She followed his gaze and glimpsed a four post bed dressed in samite with a tassled canopy. The bed invited with its luxury and sumptuous drapery. At first, she had thought the bed part of the art collection.

Alastair looked at her from head to feet. Having dried, her gown no longer clung to her curves as intimately.

"It was quite wanton of you to have dampened your gown," Alastair said, "but the effect will be much more promising if you did away with the garment."

"Here? Now?" she quizzed.

"Here," he answered nonchalantly. "And now."

"But…" Nerves came upon her as she anticipated what was to happen, that her desires were to come to fruition. "I shall lock the doors."

He stopped her. "There is no need."

"No need? But what if someone were to enter?"

"That concerns me not."

Her eyes widened.

"This is the Chateau Debauchery," he explained. "Were you not clear that all forms of debauchery occur here?"

"Yes, but…this is my *first* visit."

"You agreed to do as I bid. If you prefer to do otherwise, we may call an end to the evening. Is that what you wish?"

"No," she replied resolutely but still hesitated. Was she truly to undress before her cousin? Did he expect to call a dressing maid?

As if in answer to her question, he said, "Turn around. I shall unpin you."

Letting out a tense breath, she turned her back to him. "What—what if someone were to enter?"

He removed the first pin. "Then they may watch."

She whipped around. "Watch?"

He turned her back around. "You invited others to ogle you when you dampened your gown."

She regretted having done so. She glanced at the doors.

"Many find the witness of others titillating."

His voice had lowered, its allure beckoning the warmth in her to grow.

"I find it disconcerting," she voiced.

The bodice of her gown relaxed about her when he had removed the final pin. Her breath caught in her throat as his fingers grazed her shoulders and he slid the sleeves off her. She closed her eyes, half wondering if she were in a dream. She would have bet a thousand pounds that such a thing—

being undressed by Alastair—could come to pass.

The dress pooled at her feet. She gulped. Perhaps she ought not proceed. She was no beauty and far below the standards the marquess was undoubtedly accustomed to. He was granting a favor, his reluctance obvious. But if he had not interfered and left her to her own devices, it would be Lord Devon removing her gown. Perhaps. Perhaps she should be grateful that she was not alone. Perhaps she should take full advantage of the moment.

"Oh!" she gasped when she realized he had untied her lone petticoat.

"Do you wish to reconsider?" he asked.

"I had not thought you intended…"

"I intend you should be undressed, your body bared to me."

Once more her breath caught. Her courage faltered. Perhaps she ought not. Perhaps it were safer, wiser to call an end to the evening.

Chapter Thirteen

HE COULD HAVE PAVED THE path for her with soft kisses, rousing her desire so that she should wish to shed her garments. As she might yet reconsider, he would not go easily upon her. Her unease was palpable.

But the act of undressing a woman had an effect Alastair could not be impervious to. Her body was not unlike the full and supple nudes in the *I Modi*. The tightening at his crotch grew as he observed the swell of her rump through her shift and petticoat. There was, too, her boldness. It both vexed and impressed him. As he was not one who favored coquetry, he appreciated her directness. Her curiosity amused him. What manner of experience could he provide her? His arrogance made him doubt the stableboy could have been greatly inspiring.

Damnation.

"Turn around," he ordered.

She turned to face him, crossed her arms as if her limbs could replace her lost clothing, and pleaded once more, "Will you not consider locking the doors, my lord?"

"Ask again, and I shall *open* the doors."

She pursed her lips in dissatisfaction. "Are you to undress as well?"

"At present, no."

As if deciding to cover her lower body, she dropped her arms but knew not how to place her hands. She bent one arm and gripped the other. Not satisfied, she crossed her arms once more over her bosom and held herself near the shoulders. Her nervous movements unsettled him.

"Come."

He took her wrist and drew her to the bed. After having her stand before one of the bedposts, he untied his cravat, which he used to bind her wrists above her head to the bedpost behind her.

She tried to struggle from him. "Wait! What do you do?"

But his strength easily overcame her resistance. He secured the linen above her.

"This is most…uncommon," she remarked with some alarm.

He smirked. "Not at the Chateau Debauchery."

She flushed. "For what purpose do you tie me here? What if someone should enter and find me like this?"

He contemplated leaving her tied to the bedpost for an hour or so. It would serve the little ingrate right.

"Alastair! This is mortifying!" she continued, yanking against her restraints, but his cravat held strong. "If someone should come upon me like this—"

"They could have their way with you," he could not resist.

Her mouth dropped open. "I wish you had let me alone with Lord Devon! Surely I would have been better off in his hands."

The name disconcerted him, and Alastair closed the distance between them. "You would trust Devon over me?"

"I know for certain what *you* are like. Do you fault me for putting the odds in his favor?"

He considered the sense in what she said. Indeed, knowing little of Devon and knowing too much of him, she had made a reasonable deduction.

"Your hands were a distraction," he explained. "By removing them from your concern, you are better able to mind the pleasure."

Her breath stalled as she accepted his reasoning. Her expression softened, and once more he found he was not impervious to her. He took a step back lest his lust took the reigns.

"Do you speak truthfully?" she inquired. "This is no trickery?"

"You are not the first to be bound to a bed," he replied, "and they have all enjoyed being restrained."

She ceased pulling against the linen but asked, "But how are we to attempt—?"

He could not resist brushing back a curl of hair that had fallen before her face. She looked quite delicious tied to the bedpost. "Call upon your imagination, my dear."

She stared up at him in almost childlike wonder. The brightness of her eyes called to him and he found his resolve to make her reconsider her desires wane.

"I am ready for what you would do," she said quietly.

The huskiness of her voice made the heat flare in his veins. Perhaps it was knowing that his own satisfaction, that which he had eagerly anticipated for a sennight, was to be denied. Perhaps he was simply easily titillated, and it did not matter that the woman bent over the tabletied to the bed was Millie. Bereft of other company, perhaps any woman would have caused his desire to swell.

Her stays laced conveniently in the front. Above them, her breasts swelled enticingly. He ran his knuckles along the top of one mound and heard her breath catch. Lightly, he slid his fingers to the cleavage and then down to the ribbon. After loosening the laces, he pried the stays apart enough for the breasts to spill forward. He cupped an orb. She inhaled sharply.

It was a delicious sound, a delicious moment, knowing that such a simple touch could elicit such a reaction. He groped the supple flesh. Her lashes fluttered.

It was wrong. Wrong to manhandle his cousin in this manner, to strip her and fondle her. However, the impropriety of it was beginning to have a titillating effect. He never would've allowed himself to go this far if she had not acquiesced—even prompted him into action.

She had lovely full breasts. He passed his thumb over the nipple, making her shudder. The bud hardened further. He played with it, tugged it, rolled it between thumb and finger. She emitted a soft groan, a rumble at the back of her throat.

He palmed both breasts and gazed upon their likeness. Wicked thoughts went through his mind with what he could do to such beauties. He tried to ignore the heat churning in his groin.

Releasing her, he went to fetch a glass of water for her. The port still presided in her body, and as she had not partaken of the tea that had been brought to her room, she would require hydration. He held the glass to her lips, and she drank without protest.

"Thank you, my lord," she said after she had consumed half the glass. "I require no more."

"You will finish it."

He put the glass to her mouth. She dutifully complied, then looked to him much like a child might wait for praise or acknowledgment. Had her eyes always held so much sparkle? He found himself pulled into their depths. An odd desire to kiss her again tickled his fancy.

Resisting, he stepped away and retrieved another glass of water.

"I have had enough."

He noted that her shift had mostly dried and did not cling to her body as tightly as it had during the dinner. He had to admit the effect of the wet garments had been provocative.

"It was quite naughty of you to have dampened your gown," he remarked in a low voice.

She flushed. "Yes. I had never done so before. I promise I shall not do so again."

He leaned in toward her. "Why not? It was quite appealing."

Her breath caught.

He tipped the glass over her bosom. She gasped

when the liquid spilled over her, slowly seeping through the shift. There was not enough water to dampen the entire garment, but the fabric clung to her hips and parts of her thighs nicely.

He stepped back to admire how the water glistened upon her skin. "Now, let us proceed to the main repast."

Mildred held her breath. She trembled, but not merely from the dampness of her garments. His caresses had roused every nerve in her body. She would not have thought she could yearn for Alastair's touch as much as she did. She wanted him to kiss her again.

He did.

How delicious his lips felt against hers! Nothing tasted finer. They pressed against her with such sweetness, but with enough ardor to make her desire swell. He parted her lips with his, and his tongue grazed the insides of her mouth, making her shiver.

"Well done," he whispered against her lips.

She kissed him back, seeking more pressure from his lips. He obliged, taking mouthfuls of her and making her head swim with a euphoria she had never known. His hand went to the back of her head to hold her still as he consumed her. She arched toward him. Her belly grazed what was a definite bulge at his crotch. A victorious thrill shot through her, and she pressed herself harder against that thickness.

His fingers went through her hair, tugging slightly. She would have welcomed any manner of touch, no matter how harsh from him. A craving had engulfed her now. A craving that only he could satisfy. To signal this, she continued to kiss him despite the awkwardness of her inexperience. He tightened his hold of her hair till she gasped. He wanted her to stop. She wondered if it was because she did not kiss well.

He pulled her head back and seared his mouth to her exposed neck. She nearly wept at the waves of desire rolling through her body. There were no words to describe how marvelous his lips felt against her neck. The grazing of his tongue tickled and thrilled. He suckled her neck, causing the tension between her legs to double—nay, triple.

Take me. Please take me.

At that moment, she wanted him more than she had ever wanted anything else. Her body bowed off the post, pulling at the binding. It was madness how much she needed him, madness how the heat engulfing her could elicit such divine agitation, a pleasure that drove her to distraction. He clasped a buttock, and another wave of heat bowled through her. She rubbed herself harder against him, the pressure inside her body needing to meet with an equal pressure outside.

With a groan, he shoved his hips at her. She had not thought it possible for the bulge between his legs to harden further. With a vigor that surprised her, she ground herself wantonly against him. A small part of her mind cautioned what he must think of her behavior, but she paid it no heed.

At present, she wanted only to relieve the fire consuming her and feared that at any moment, Alastair might come to his senses and withdraw.

Instead, he pushed back against her as he continued to mouth her neck, her jaw, her mouth. Her hips, however, he tilted toward his pelvis. Desire swam through her. There could not be a more divine place than where she was, trapped between the wooden post and his equally hard body. She wanted to speak his name or a word to indicate she was ready and willing.

He groped a breast, kneading the flesh with his fingers. She winced and gasped as her sensitive nipples grazed against him. But she had never felt more alive. She needed and wanted to merge her body to this man who could inflict such acute sensations and coax such delicious wonders. The combination enthralled her to a height she had never before known.

At long last, his hand was between her legs, stoking where the flame burned hottest. She would have preferred his bare fingers but was too aroused to mind her shift scraping against her. The friction from the garment produced a different but still pleasing sensation. With each and every stroke, the fire grew. The rapturous agitation reverberated through her body, and she doubted that she could contain its explosion. She had no wish to contain it. If the euphoria building within her did not find release, she would go mad.

She pressed herself into his hand. He quickened his motions.

And then it happened. What she had sought, what she had craved for the longest time. What she might never experience ever again.

The pressure inside her exploded, shooting shudders through her entire frame. She bucked against him, against the post. Her body exalted in the rapture, but could it survive its victory? Should it stretch or curl into itself? Should she tense or relax? As she waffled between the various responses, the euphoria continued to ripple through her and ricochet between her thighs till she thought she could endure no more. She sobbed as her body quivered and quivered and quivered.

Chapter Fourteen

WATCHING HER SPEND AND HEAR-
ING her cries had caused his ardor to swell.
Alastair knew when she had spent, the moment she
had reached the apex of euphoria, but he had continued to strum his fingers between her thighs that
she might never forget the depth of sensations her
body was capable of.

She gave another cry and her body jerked against
the bedpost. The blood pounded everywhere in
his body, and especially at his groin. Damn. His
body wanted very much to take her. She looked
and sounded far too becoming. The scent of her
arousal wafted through his nostrils, and the primal
urges soared within him. He doubted she would
protest. He had seen the plea in her eyes earlier.
She had wanted him to ravish her.

Millie. Millie. Millie.

But the woman whose body trembled against
his, her breasts spilling from her stays, her quim
sopping wet, was not the cousin he had known.
This woman who had ground herself at his cock

with a desperation no whore could replicate was a surprise, was intoxicating, was provocative.

She let out a haggard moan and, reluctantly, he withdrew his hand. He took a step away from her, putting space between their bodies and hoping that, in doing so, he could calm the heat raging inside him.

Her body slumped against the post as she found her breath.

His hand itched to rub himself. She was an amazing sight upon the bed. He cleared his throat. "You are quite lovely when you spend, Millie. "

She looked up at him, her eyes shining uncommonly bright. His praise had pleased her.

"What may I do for you, Alastair?"

He growled, for he did not like the sound of his name. It reminded him of their relation and of his responsibility. Katherine had asked him to care for someone. Circumstances made Millie his selection, and though he had had honorable intentions at the beginning, what had he ended up doing instead? Disrobed and fondled her. He truly was an unredeemable cad.

""How do you, er, take your satisfaction?" she inquired.

"You need not worry yourself of that."

"But…" She lowered her gaze to his crotch.

He adjusted himself in front of her so that his erection was less apparent.

"It seems only fair," she added.

Her words were like the call of sirens, but he grumbled, "I can take care of myself."

"I should be happy to perform a similar service, as you had provided me with…with completion."

"You have not earned such a privilege," he replied, needing to put an end to their dialogue.

"Do you not wish to spend?"

He narrowed his eyes at her. "We are done with this discussion."

He stepped to her to undo the bonds from her wrists.

She looked up at him. "Would you like for me to suck your cock?"

He froze. *What the hell had she said?*

"I am told that all men enjoy it greatly."

He stared down at her, hardly able to believe his ears. Had she truly said the word "cock?" If so, his wanton little cousin was far bawdier than he could ever have imagined.

He put his hands to his hips. "Did that stableboy tell you this? I will have his name," he demanded, thinking that he would have to beat the pup to a bloody pulp.

"What does it matter?" she returned. "It is true, is it not?"

"Did he force you to take his member?"

"By 'member,' you mean to say 'cock?'"

A vein in his neck throbbed. "Such a vulgar word should not pass the lips of a refined young lady."

She had the audacity to roll her eyes. "Have you not determined that I am far from a proper miss?"

"Did the bastard force you?"

"I *wanted* his cock! I was curious. And it pleased me to pleasure him in this fashion."

"Undoubtedly, he suggested it. Who is he?"

"No one of consequence. But, as I have had some practice in it, I think you will find pleasure in my performance."

Hell and damnation. He was being propositioned by his cousin—once more.

"I have defiled you enough," he answered, and reached his cravat.

"Or you can take me. Here. Now. I beg of you. Make use of my body. Lest I am not to your liking."

He suppressed an oath. "Millie, that is not the issue."

"But it must be. You have not disavowed it. Your arousal is quite plain, but you must not desire my body enough."

"Millie! Do you forget we are cousins?"

"Not blood cousins. And no one need know. Please let me satisfy you. It would gratify me to do so."

He groaned as his erection stretched at her words and he hoped he could answer without wavering. "I can address my own needs to satisfaction."

"I know I must not please as well as Miss Hollingsworth, but you could close your eyes and imagine you are with her, and not your inferior cousin."

The blood was pounding in his head, clouding all thought.

"I'll not mind. You could—"

He succumbed. He crushed his lips to hers. To silence her. To ease the all-consuming pressure at his crotch. To prove that she was not as undesirable as she thought. To surrender.

And once he gave himself permission to proceed, he knew there was no turning back.

The more he tasted her, the finer she became.

Over and over, his mouth ravaged hers. He kissed for *his* pleasure now, and it seemed would have done so even had she not invited him. Fisting his hand in her hair, he tilted her head in various directions, that he could sample all angles of her mouth. How delectably warm and moist she was. That she had no skill in the art of kissing mattered not. Her efforts amused him, and he favored them over no effort at all.

The air between them grew as hot as that in the hearth. Her breasts pressed into him. Her hips. The little wanton had ground herself hungrily at him, and he had nearly succumbed the first time she had displayed the depths of her prurience. How could a woman who hitherto had shown such reserve, relinquish all inhibition?

He flattered himself that he was the inspiration, though Millie had never shown any partiality toward him. It was what made him part with the sort of respect that he rarely spared his fellow men. She was not one of the many simpering maids who melted at his touch or tried to earn his affection through coquetry or flattery. Neither was she as beautiful, as witty, or as charming. But she was, for the most part, a sensible young woman, without artifice and possessed of a daring spirit. He had not anticipated this last quality, and the mystery of it intrigued him.

His desire yearned to burst free of its confines. He fought the urgency and shoved his hips at her, giving her time and a sense of what she asked for. If she had a change of heart, despite the difficulty of fighting a tide turned, he would withdraw. But only upon her word.

Had she truly surrendered her maidenhead to the damned stablehand? He did not think Millie would lie to him, but what if she had overstated what had happened?

"If you wish to reconsider," he muttered between kisses.

"Damn it, Alastair," she huffed. "Hang your qualms."

Bloody hell. He reached beneath her shift and went straight for the treasure trove. His fingers thrummed her clitoris, then pried between the folds. She gasped as they intruded into her sanctity.

Damn. She was tight. Tight as a virgin. And wet. Steaming wet. Nothing could be more enticing. With surprising gentleness and patience, he pushed his fingers farther inside. She squirmed beneath him and purred. She had better not be a virgin.

But even if she was, he doubted that he could retreat. His arousal raged too strongly now.

His fingers grazed that most favored ally—that wrinkled pearl, still swollen, protruding from between her folds—before curling inside her quim.

"Heavens," she breathed.

He fondled her till he had her panting and desperate. His own arousal was reaching its peak, fueled by the wet heat embracing his fingers. He had to sample this lusciousness with another part of his body.

"Alastair…" she moaned.

This time he favored the sound of his name upon her lips.

He released her hair and unbuttoned his fall. His

erection sprang forward, hard and at the ready. He looked to her to see if he could detect fear or hesitation but saw none. Instead, she licked her bottom lip!

Holy...

"Pray, make me wait no longer," she said.

Her words ignited him. He threw up her shift and, holding her by the backs of her thighs, he pressed the crown of his shaft to her nether lips. It took all his forbearance not to sink himself into her.

"Yes! Yes!" she gasped.

He felt her flex herself about his tip. No further encouragement was required. He sheathed himself into her, her wetness providing easy passage.

She cried out and stiffened. And for a moment, he worried that perhaps she *was* a virgin. But his worries were muted by the glory surrounding his cock, pulsing into his loins. She was marvelous. Pure delight.

He lowered his head to capture her lips and trail soft kisses from ear to temple. After she had relaxed, she writhed as if seeking motion. Slowly, he began to thrust.

"*Ohhh...*"

Her lashes fluttered. Her back arched. He settled himself a little deeper. Damn. Her womanhood felt as impressive as any he had sampled before. It was all he could do not to ram himself full and deep into her. With sighs and grunts, she writhed between him and the post, the movement of her body driving him wild. He shoved his hips at her to pin her in place so that he could slide more of him inside her. He curled the fingers of one hand into hers while he held onto the bedpost with the other. He ground himself into her with long strokes that left her breath haggard and her body trembling. When she began to grunt in earnest, he quickened his pace.

"Yes! Oh, yes!" she cried.

In her position, there was little she could do to match his thrusting, but he was more than content to do all the work. The bed rattled with the force of his motions. He saw her eyes rolled toward the back of her head, her brow furrowed and her jaw slackened by passion. He intensified his pounding, shoving his full length up into her. His cods boiled, but he held the fire in check.

She filled the room with her cries and incoherent words, and then her wail split the air as her body convulsed and bucked, submitting to that carnal euphoria. He speared himself into her wet heat, seeking the same. She trembled violently against him, but he required a few more thrusts before he, too, reached his apex.

He pulled out of her as quickly as he could before his seed shot forth. His cods pumped the fire through him, draining his desire onto the floor below. He shivered when a second wave of seed poured forth. He clutched himself to ease the last drop, then shook his head to release the tension that had clamped the whole of his body.

When the storm had finally passed, his breathing had returned to normalcy, he looked down to find her gazing up at him, her cheeks flushed, her lips still parted.

Dear God. What had he done?

Chapter Fifteen

IT WAS NOT WHAT MILDRED wanted to see.
Moments before, she had savored his growl,
his shivers as he found his own release. Her own
had thrilled, astounded, delighted her to no end.
She had never before felt such divine intensity, had
wondered if her body might implode or explode.
Every second had been a wonder. His strength as
he had bucked her against the post; his stamina in
pumping his hardness up into her, maintaining an
angle that drew the most beautiful heat through
her loins; his expression when he gazed down
upon her. She had not felt her plain self. Even if he
took her merely because he had no other option
available to him—undoubtedly he had only the
most utilitarian use for her body—the joining of
their bodies excited her. She had relished it all.

But not the guilt she saw in his eyes. The regret.
It would ruin the beauty of what had transpired
betwixt them. She could not let it happen.

"Thank you, Alastair, thank you," she said. "I
hope it was as pleasurable for you as it was for me."

"There would not be the evidence of it upon
the floor if it were not the case," he said, his voice

low and slightly hoarse. He looked her in the eyes as he untied her wrists. "Was it pleasurable for you?"

"Exceedingly."

"Truly? I think I was overly harsh in my motions. Sometimes it is hard to contain the force of the carnal."

"I welcome it."

He grimaced and pulled away to replace his fall. "I ought not have—"

"That would not be in accordance with the purpose of Château Follet I pray you suffer no regrets," she added as she rubbed her wrists, a little sore from being bound. "I will lose all respect for you if you do."

"What of you? Will you regret?"

"Not at all."

"You will think differently tomorrow."

"Why ask me if you are so certain that you know the answer to your own question?"

He stared at her, then a smile appeared. He looked down at her stays. "Allow me."

She stepped back. "Are we done already?"

He was visibly taken aback by her question but answered, "Yes, we are done."

She glanced down at her breasts, recalling how he had looked upon them with desire. "But I had hoped to take your member."

"Millie...did you think we were engaged in something other than congress?"

"Into my mouth."

His eyes steeled, and he pressed his lips into a firm line. "I will not degrade you further."

"But there is titillation in degradation, is there

not? Is it not supremely wanton and wicked to take that man's part and place it where nature had not intended?"

"Millie, the hour is late."

"Do you not enjoy the act?"

"Millie, I will not allow you to browbeat me into this."

"Browbeat? No. I merely wish to entice you. I have received some instruction in this and am no novice."

He shook his head. "Good God, Millie. When I discover this wretch who has turned you…"

"Turned me 'what?' Into you?"

He looked a little as if he might like to throttle her. "I will ask no more of you after this," she promised.

"You are asking to—to take me into your mouth…"

She gave him a broad smile. "Yes. Please. My lord."

He uttered an oath beneath his breath. Before he could answer, she had sunk to her knees before him. She eyed his crotch hungrily.

"You might even be pleasantly surprised," she said. "I may be as good as or better than Miss Hollingsworth might have been."

She reached a hand to the buttons of his fall, but he caught her wrist.

"Millie—"

She pouted. "Come. It is not as if we are engaging in sin."

"Not engaging in sin?" he exclaimed, incredulous.

"Further sin. We have done the worst of it

already."

With her other hand, she cupped his groin. He groaned. Could she tempt him once more? The prospect that she could, that she was capable of such sway, excited her.

"I am not one given to generous doses of conscience," he said, "and you would lay to waste my attempts at goodness."

"I never invited you to be what you are not."

He paused. Perhaps he appreciated this in her. Doubtlessly, the women who hoped to tempt a proposal from him would not wish him to continue as he was once wed.

"I pray you be the rake with me," she said as she pressed her lips to him. "It is only fair."

With her one free hand, she undid a button. With a shaky breath, he released her other hand. She rubbed her hands over him, coaxing him to hardness once more. A thrill went through her when she felt him responding.

She finished off all the buttons and freed his erection. It was glorious. All this hardness for and because of her. She brushed her fingers over the ridges of the veins and shivered. This had been inside her, had penetrated her deeper than anything had. Eagerly, she licked its underside, her tongue finding a spot that made him moan.

"You've no need to do anything, Millie," he said.

"You granted and fulfilled my wishes and sacrificed your night to do right by me, but do not assume that I am merely returning your favor. I take much pleasure in the taste of cockmeat."

She engulfed him. He gave a quivering moan.

She knew not if she tasted him, her, or the both of them upon his flesh. Heat swirled between her legs at the notion that she might be ingesting the flavor of her own desire. What wickedness!

Greedily, she sank her mouth farther down his shaft.

"Dear God."

Pleased at his reaction, she attempted to swallow more of him. With the stable hand, she had been able to take her mouth all the way to his pelvis. With Alastair, several inches still separated her lips from the base of his erection. She combed her fingers through the curls at his crotch, then cupped his sack, cradling the heavy balls there. He grunted and wound a hand through her hair.

She knew to keep her teeth behind her lips and slowly began the motion that his sex adored. She drew her mouth up his length, then down as far as she could go. Over and over, she slid herself along his manhood. She sucked at the flared crown.

"Ahhh…" he gasped, his grasp on her tightening.

His hand at the back of her head, he pushed her back down. She went farther than she had done before and gagged when his tip grazed the back of her throat. After recovering, she gripped his member with both hands to keep it steady. But he dictated the pace. He pulled her up his shaft, then pressed her back down. In response, she sucked him as hard as she could, lapping at him with her tongue. She might not be the most skilled paramour he had ever had, but she would demonstrate she could be the most ravenous. She wanted him to remember her, to remember this night and not feel as if he had been jilted, but recall it fondly.

"Bloody hell," he murmured. He matched her vivacity and pumped her head up and down. She took as much of him as she could. It was not always elegant, but by the thrusting of his hips, she could tell that his arousal was growing by leaps and bounds—and very quickly. She gagged often but recovered each time. She came close to taking all of him and hoped he was not disappointed that she might not be as skilled as he had hoped.

He popped his member from her mouth. It glistened with her saliva. Before she could protest, he had scooped her up, carrying her to the bed. He lay her down and clamped his mouth over hers as he removed his waistcoat and kicked off his shoes. After his kisses had left her breathless, he pulled down his braces and swept off his shirt. She eyed the toned shape of his nakedness. It was beautiful and as inspiring as any work of art. Ardor soared between her thighs.

He made quick work of his remaining garments before attending to hers. He untied her stays completely and fondled her breasts, playfully pinching her nipples. He pulled the shift and stays down her arms, kissing the exposed skin as he went along. She wanted to return to her earlier feast, to see if she might be able to coax him to spend into her mouth, but he clearly had other plans. As long as it involved no regrets, she would not object. In resolving to stay at Château Follet, she had resolved to have none, and would tolerate none in him.

His body hovering over hers, he planted soft kisses upon her upper thighs. She was consumed with desire all over again. She pulled at him, wanting to mate her mouth to his, wanting him to cover her body with his weight.

"Behave yourself," he warned with a light slap to her breast.

She pursed her lips in displeasure but obeyed. He parted her thighs and situated himself between her legs. His gaze was *there*, where wetness still prevailed. What did he intend, she wondered?

He fingered her slit, then caressed the little bud of flesh that was so easily excited. Before long, she was moaning and writhing. His fondling was delightful, but she wanted more. She wanted to be filled. His fingers inside of her might do but not as well as that other part of him. It was made to fit inside of her.

Withdrawing his finger, he replaced the digit with his mouth.

Her body jumped, and he put a hand upon her pelvis to hold her in place.

Merciful heavens.

He had his tongue *there*. And it was...it was beyond delicious. Her mind reeled to think—to know—that he tasted her most intimate parts. She supposed it differed little from the bawdiness of taking cock into her mouth, but she wondered how he must perceive the scent and the wetness down there. He seemed not to mind, for his tongue continued its exploration, and when it found a spot that elicited a sharp gasp from her, bore down harder upon its discovery. She clutched at the thin bedclothes beneath.

Merciful heavens.

Enchantment rippled from her groin. She

glanced only briefly at him to see the dark locks of his head bobbing between her legs. Shutting her eyes, she allowed her head to fall back upon the bed and gave herself to the apogee his ministrations coaxed. She twisted the bedsheet in her fingers when the prospect of rapture grew too much for her to contain.

He shifted his caresses to give her a respite before taking her swollen bud into his mouth and sucking till her back arched off the bed.

"Alastair!"

He pinched the bud he had teased to glory. His tongue found a new spot of weakness, and attacked it vigorously. Soon she was panting and clenching her body against the onslaught.

"I think I shall spend again…"

"Not yet, my dear. With forbearance, you may increase the pleasure that awaits."

But she could not. In the face of so much pleasure engulfing her, she could not hold back the tide. It tore through her, shaking her legs and making her cry out. Every lick, every caress made her tremble.

When at last he stopped to allow her to bathe in the aftermath of her finish, he climbed atop her, and she felt his hardness at her entry. He hesitated for a moment, so she wrapped her arms about him and pulled him down to her.

"Thank you," she whispered, then angled her hips at him.

He gave a low grunt and pushed himself in, filling her. In their present position, his shaft slid into her easily, as nature had intended. Her quim had been fashioned for his member, and she marveled at the thickness throbbing inside of her.

Her first time, the insertion of that part had caused intense pain, and there had been some discomfort when Alastair had entered her earlier, but she had quickly adjusted, and that discomfort had melted into the greatest pleasure her body could know. Indeed, she sought the discomfort now and moved her hips to welcome more of him.

Understanding the wordless invitation, he buried himself to the hilt. She purred her satisfaction.

His thrusts were gradual and slow, but her arousal was quick and sure. The prior flame of desire had not yet been extinguished, and she would have gladly spent again. She met his movements, engaged with him as if it were a dance, a dance of undulations, of two becoming one.

Wanting to join more of herself to him, she pulled him down farther and raised her head so that she could kiss him. He seemed surprised at first but readily availed himself of her mouth. Her hunger intensified, she would have taken every part of his body into hers if she could. As if sensing this, he rolled his hips into her at a quicker pace. She ground herself at him in response.

Parting from her mouth, he propped himself up so that he could delve his shaft deeper into her. She grasped his arms and attempted to greet the faster thrusts with her own, but she could not keep up. That irresistible tension roiled once more. She writhed, attempting to stem it from boiling over, for she would have him spend before her. But she had not even time to ask his permission before rapture overtook her. It shattered her body, drowning her in heated bliss.

Chapter Sixteen

H E WAS UNDONE BY HER sob, the clenching of her quim, and the spasms of her limbs. With his own body falling into that tantalizing paroxysm, Alastair withdrew before the pressure raging inside of him shot forth, though his seed sprayed onto her belly before he could direct it elsewhere. He tried to contain the shudders from collapsing him atop her as pleasure ripped up and down his legs. When the last of his seed had been milked from him, he remained hovering above her to catch his breath.

Looking down at her, he realized he had been undone minutes earlier when their gazes had locked. The bloom of her earlier orgasm and the flush of desire renewed, mixed with a look of wonder, had pushed him past the point of no return. Seeing the furrow of her brow, knowing that euphoria approached for them both, was the most scintillating moment.

Lowering himself, he kissed her brow before rolling off of her. She caught his arm before he left the bed to fetch linen.

"Thank you, Andre—Alastair."

He would have allowed her the use of his name. Taking her hand from him, he kissed it and smiled at her. He glanced down at the emission sliding from her belly.

"Your pardon," he said.

She followed his gaze, and an impish smile hovered about her lips. He stayed the temptation to kiss her again and went to the sideboard, where he found linen in one of the drawers. He wet the linen in a basin of water. Returning, he cleansed her belly and her thighs. She might not have the most perfect form, but, with her unblemished skin, she was worthy of painting.

"Thank you," she said again.

There was a captivating sparkle to her eyes, and he gave in to the temptation. He tilted her chin and took her lips, admiring their soft fullness. She gave a contented sigh after they parted. He went to pour her a glass of water, but when he turned to face the bed, he found her stretched upon the bed, her head upon the pillow and her eyes closed.

He covered her with the bedclothes. Climbing into bed beside her, he let out his breath. A part of him wondered that he had taken matters as far as he had, but once he had entered the vortex, he had found his cousin more alluring than he had ever expected. He was glad that she had enjoyed the evening, but would she wake with regrets in the morning? Should he renew his scolding—and add Katherine to his admonitions?

He fell asleep before putting his questions to bed.

When his cousin awoke the following morrow, it was nearly noon. She opened her eyes to find him fully dressed. He had been sitting in a chair, viewing her as she slept, still in amazement of what had happened last night. He had a whole new appreciation for Millie.

Poor Millie. Her misery over her engagement to Haversham was greater than Alastair had cared to understand. It took courage to venture to a place such as the château to honor the carnal cravings inside her. He would never have guessed that she had already compromised herself, but it did not diminish his admiration for her spirit. But now that the port had worn off, would the light of day bring with it the remorse he had sought to save her from?

"Good morning, Millie," he greeted, and rose from his chair to ring for a servant.

She flushed. "Good morning, er, my lord."

"How do you fare?"

She shifted beneath the blanket. "Well, my lord."

He resisted taking a seat on the bed and returned to his chair. "I will have breakfast brought to you—or lunch, if you prefer."

She sat up, drawing the blanket over her bosom. "Lunch! Good gracious, what time is it?"

"The noon hour."

"Heavens! I never sleep this late!"

He smiled. "You did have a strenuous night."

"Yes, I did," she said slowly.

He expected the repentance to emerge at this time, but, instead, she smiled and looked at him. "Thanks to you."

He cleared his throat and crossed one leg over the other to contain the surge of tension at his crotch.

"You have no regrets?" he asked.

"I am fully content with what has transpired."

"You will think differently with time."

"You are presumptuous, sir."

"There are few who would dare speak to me in such a manner, and fewer who could do so without raising my ire."

He was tempted to teach her more courtesy. A spanking might do.

She lowered her gaze for a few seconds. "Your pardon, but, really, Alastair, you do not know me well enough to make such a claim. In truth, I am quite surprised that *you* seem to harbor more shame than I."

The thought seemed to amuse her, and he bristled. "I was only worried for your sake. My sex can dispense with guilt much more easily than yours, especially over matters of the flesh."

She was silent in thought. "Am I more the wanton jade if I harbor no repentance or shame? Am I a...slut?"

He groaned, and he felt another unsettling tug at his crotch. He had thought such sensations would not have persisted past the night.

"Millie, that is not at all what I intended with my words! I applaud that you honored the natural cravings inside you and sought to fulfill them without fear."

"You tried to stop me."

"That was before I knew you had already forsaken your virtue!"

"Then you have no need to worry of me, though I appreciate your concern. It is quite hopeful that you may not be as unredeemable as society deems you to be."

He growled at her teasing smile. Women. If he had had a choice, he would have selected one of his own sex to fulfill Katherine's birthday wish.

"My dear cousin," Millie said. "I will forever be grateful to you for last night. My one fear is that you will henceforth be awkward in my presence."

"You think our relationship can remain the same after what happened?"

"Why not?"

"Your naivety is charming at best."

She pursed her lips. "Well, we are not often in each other's company. I expect it will be even less once I am Mrs. Haversham. The night will hold little significance for you after you have had a tumble with Miss Hollingsworth or whomever you choose next. I daresay you will have forgotten the night altogether after your next visit here."

He rather hoped this would be the case. Theirs had been an easy interaction till yesterday, and he now believed he enjoyed her company as much as he could enjoy the company of anyone.

"And what of you?" he asked. "You blushed at a mere greeting of 'good morning' from me."

"I did? Well, that will not always be the case."

He did not refute her wishful thinking and rose to attend the knock at the door. Bhadra held a tray of tea, toast, and eggs. She bobbed a curtsy before entering.

"Lady Katherine is just arrived," Bhadra said to Millie. "Shall I bring items of dress down here?"

"You may bring Miss Abbey a robe and dress her in the comfort of her chambers," he instructed. "I will attend my aunt."

"I pray you will not be cross with her," Millie said quickly.

He gave her an admonishing look for speaking in front of a servant. Chastened, she fixed upon the toast before her. He held the door for Bhadra before following her.

"Where is Lady Katherine?" he asked the maid.

"In the red drawing room with Madame Follet."

He made for the drawing room, bowed upon his entry to the two women, who seemed engaged in quite the feminine intrigue, and addressed Marguerite. "May I have a word with my aunt?"

He could see Marguerite hesitate, but his tone would not be denied.

"*Bien sur, mon cheri*," she said. Before whisking herself away, she bid Katherine make Follet her second home, as she had once done.

"You look well, Andre," Katherine remarked with feigned nonchalance when they were alone.

He put his hands on his hips. "You set it up on purpose."

It seemed she suppressed a smile. "Whatever do you mean?"

"The promise you exacted from me on your birthday. Then, bringing Millie to Château Follet. My God, bringing Millie to Château Follet! What were you thinking?"

His aunt was not intimidated. "Take care of

your tone, Andre."

"Your actions merit more than a stern tone, and do not suppose just because you are my aunt that I will refrain from—"

She beamed. "My, my! You care for your cousin much more than I thought possible."

He frowned.

"That you would risk affronting *me* in order to protect her concerns," Katherine explained.

"*You* put me in such a position."

"You could have elected to go about your own affairs."

"Have you forgotten the rogues and rakes that abound here?"

"I adore the greatest one of them all, and perhaps *you* have forgotten that I married one!"

"Richard was a rarity. And it was foolish of you to have staked Millie's reputation on my having a conscience."

"First of all, Millie and Château Follet are perfectly suited to each other."

"How long have you been cognizant of her past?"

"For quite some time. Saw it with my own eyes. Poor creature was absolutely mortified," Katherine continued, "but it was truly the best thing to have happened for her. And as you would not rescind her dowry, I thought she should make the most of her last days as a bachelorette."

"By taking her to Château Follet!"

"Did she not enjoy herself? *That* would be my greatest regret."

"Not that she might have destroyed her reputation? That would be a sure way to expel

Haversham."

"There is little chance that Millie will be discovered."

"You risk too much, my lady."

"I commend your concerns on behalf of your cousin. Marguerite told me you were quite insufferable last night in your attempts to whisk Millie to safety. I knew there was good to be found in you. But you were not successful in your attempts."

"Because I could find no woman of reason."

"That is not impediment enough for you."

"Marguerite refused my request for her carriage."

"But you did not press her a second time?"

"She threatened to throw me out! As long as Millie was kept safe, it was just as well that we did not attempt to travel at night."

"And did you? Keep her safe?"

He shook his head. Women, once fixed upon an item, could be as relentless as the bite of a ferret. "I forbid you to bring Millie back to Château Follet," he said.

"I vow I will not aid and abet in adultery. But as she had already forsaken her virginity, my only hope was to provide her one night of delight, where her desires could be met in a way that a lifetime of nights with Haversham will not."

He bristled in discomfort.

"I hope you did not destroy her one opportunity?" Katherine tried again, but she received no satisfaction.

If Millie elected to confide in Katherine, that was her prerogative, but he would not divulge the events of last night.

"Millie is having breakfast but should be ready shortly thereafter," he said.

"Are you staying the remainder of the weekend?"

"Why should I not?"

"You could escort us to Bath."

"You know I have no fondness for Bath."

"No, but I thought…"

"I think you overestimate the good in me."

She sighed. "I suppose. Can you fault me for trying? I am fond of you, goodness knows why, and of dear Millie. She is a singular young woman, is she not? And much more than meets the eye."

His anger placated by his aunt's assurances that she would not be bringing Millie back to Château Follet, he became mildly amused at her efforts at matchmaking.

"She is that," he acknowledged, ignoring her frown, for she had clearly hoped for more of a response. He made a bow and took his leave, promising himself that, in the future, he would be a lot more careful in granting birthday wishes.

Chapter Seventeen

"IT EXCEEDED ALL EXPECTATION," MIL-
DRED said after she had embraced Lady
Katherine. Having completed her dress, she was
finishing the last of her packing that Bhadra had
begun last night. "It was a night I shall not forget."

Lady Katherine took a seat. "I am thrilled to
hear it. But tell me, if you will, who has made it
so memorable for you?"

Mildred blushed. "You would not believe it,
my lady, and I would not hesitate to tell you save
that…he may wish to preserve his anonymity."

"You mean Andre?"

Mildred's eyes widened. "He told you?"

Lady Katherine straightened, but there was no
vexation in her voice. "He scolded me, is what
he did. He admonished me for bringing you here
in the first place, then explained that he had to
keep you safe from the other rogues and rakes.
I gathered then that he must have been in your
company for most of the night. And as you have
revealed that it was an unforgettable night, well,

my conclusion was an easy one to draw."

Mildred eyed Lady Katherine carefully, looking for signs of disapproval, but found instead a mischievous twinkle in her eyes. "Did you know that he was going to be here?"

Lady Katherine drew in a breath. "In truth, I did. What he would do, I knew not. But I suspected he would not allow his cousin to fall in harm's way."

"You would be the only person to hazard such a thing! I don't think anyone would have bet upon Alastair having a conscience."

Lady Katherine smiled. "Surprised you, didn't he? Well, I did see to the boy's upbringing. I didn't do the best of jobs at it, but I don't think I was a total failure either."

Mildred did not know whether she ought to be sick to her stomach. Though she and Alastair were cousins, she was still much beneath his station. Would Lady Katherine truly condone a venereal relationship between them?

"I knew you would find your heart's desire at Château Follet," her ladyship continued, "and I hoped it would be Alastair who provided it to you."

"Truly?"

"Are you appalled, my dear?"

"Not appalled but surprised."

"Are you so certain you would not have wagered upon his decency?"

"He wanted, at first, to act honorably." Mildred sank onto the bed. "Till I browbeat him into feeling sorry for me."

"Dear Millie, Andre does what Andre wants."

"But I was quite insufferable! And a little inebriated. I cannot recall all that I had said. You would have been proud of his resistance. My behavior must have been monstrously intolerable and wore him down."

Lady Katherine was quiet for a moment before responding, "Well, he deserved all of it. Had he been agreeable and granted your wish on the matter of the dowry, none of this would have come to pass."

Now it was Mildred's turn at silence. Now that last night had come to pass, she did not regret his rejection of her request. Would she trade all that had happened last night for freedom from an unwanted engagement?

She shook her head. It was madness that such a question should even find pause before an answer!

"What is it, child?" her ladyship inquired. "You appear pensive. What troubles you?"

"My cousin is convinced that I will come to regret what has happened."

"Will you?"

Mildred shook her head. "Only if it irrevocably harms our kinship, but I do not see how, lest *he* suffers from regret and shame."

"I cannot see those sentiments attaching themselves to Andre."

"I shall not see us differently and shall continue to have the same regard as I have always shown my cousin."

Only now she knew him *intimately*. She had seen him naked, had held his most private member in her *mouth*, had joined her body to his in congress.

"Well, it will be a *little* different," Lady Katherine

said.

Mildred grew warm. "Yes. I—I think I had consumed one too many glasses of port or I would never have considered—not with Alastair."

"He may be a rogue, but he is a handsome one."

"Without the port, I would not have had the courage! And it did not occur to me till last night to see him in that...that *way*."

"No?"

"I think not, though..."

She wondered if she would ever forget how the look of ardor had sent such thrills through her, how she had lost herself in his kiss, and how she had bared her soul—her deepest desires—to him.

"And now that you have, you have fallen a little in love with him," Lady Katherine pronounced.

Mildred shook her head. "He is my cousin."

"Any woman who submits herself to Andre falls in love with him. You would not be mortal if you did not, my dear."

"Perhaps a little then," Mildred conceded.

"Goodness knows if I were not his aunt and were a few years younger, I should like nothing more than to have that man ravish me."

"Lady Katherine!" Mildred gasped.

Her ladyship chuckled. Mildred smiled.

"Thank you, my lady," Mildred said. "Thank you for the most marvelous adventure I will know."

"Do not make such a sweeping proclamation yet. Who knows? Perhaps you can entice Haversham to pay a visit to Château Follet?"

The suggestion struck Mildred as ludicrous, but then, Alastair must have had a similar impression of *her*, and she had astonished him a great deal. Perhaps she should not be so quick to judge her fiancé?

Mildred smiled. "Perhaps."

After taking lunch with Madame Follet, Mildred and Lady Katherine readied themselves for the continuation of their travels. Their carriage had been sent for, and as they received their coat and gloves, Mildred heard her alias called.

"Miss Abbey!"

She turned to see Lord Devon. Lady Katherine was engaged in speaking with Madame Follet, and Mildred decided not to interrupt them with introductions.

"Lord Devon," she greeted.

"It is a shame you have to leave already," he said. He lowered his voice. "I searched for you last evening."

"Your pardon. I had had every intention of returning—I did return to the assembly room, only to find it empty."

"I had given up hope that you would return and was fairly convinced that you had chosen other company."

Before Mildred could respond, a voice intervened. "She did."

They both looked in the direction of Alastair. Devon frowned as her cousin approached them.

That would not be quite true, Mildred thought

to say.

"My loss then," Devon said. He bowed to Mildred. "I hope you enjoyed your visit to Château Follet—enough to visit a second time."

Alastair looked as if he would very much like to give Devon the boot, but the Viscount withdrew.

"I still do not understand why you dislike such an amiable fellow," she said to Alastair but was glad to see him before she left. "Have you come to admonish or warn me one last time?"

He drew in a long breath. "I came to tell you that I have reconsidered your request."

"My request?" For a moment, she thought she had asked him for more of what had occurred last night.

"Concerning your dowry. I have decided to add the condition that I must approve any engagement, as well as any settlements, for the dowry to qualify."

She stared at him. Did he jest? No, he was not the sort of man given to jesting. When she was fairly certain that she had heard correctly, she said, "My lord...thank you, but I am engaged already."

"I fear any misunderstanding was my error. I had not made my condition known to your father but will make it now. Have your father bring Mr. Haversham, whom I met but briefly, to meet with me once more."

"And you will...?"

"I have a better understanding of the sort of man who would make Miss Abbott a suitable husband."

She had the urge to embrace her cousin. "Thank you! Thank you, Alastair!"

He bowed.

"Well, Andre!" Lady Katherine declared. "Are you riding with us to Bath?"

"Only to see you safely to your destination, m'lady, as you have no other escort."

"Fabulous! We will wait for your horse to be sent for."

Alastair bowed again and went to make arrangements with his valet.

"*Mon dieu!* He is not quite the scoundrel in your presence," Madame Follet remarked first to Lady Katherine, then to Mildred, "Nor yours, *mademoiselle.*"

All his more tender moments flashed before Mildred.

"It is lovely to see how our sex can inspire the better parts in men," Madame Follet added.

"I can claim no credit," Mildred replied, looking at Lady Katherine. "I think his aunt must have all to do with it."

"I?" Lady Katherine responded. "I merely acquainted you with the wonders of Château Follet. The rest was up to you."

They did not have to wait long for Alastair. Soon Mildred and Lady Katherine were ensconced in the carriage, with Alastair astride his horse beside the vehicle.

Mildred looked out the window at Château Follet. It was a place that held great significance for Lady Katherine, for she had met her husband here, and for Mildred, it would occupy a special place in her heart and mind as well. Within its walls, she had been taken to such heights as she could not have imagined.

As the carriage pulled away, Mildred considered that perhaps Lady Katherine would prove correct. Perhaps this was not to be her last adventure.

The End

More reading awaits…

Mildred's journey continues in
TEMPTING A MARQUESS FOR CHRISTMAS
(available November 2017)

THE MARQUESS OF ALASTAIR HAS doubled the dowry he is providing Miss Abbott because the sooner she is married, the sooner she is out of his care — and his fantasies.

To Mildred Abbott's dismay, her dowry is now attracting numerous unwanted suitors, and she has no interest in marrying. What she wants is an encore of her night at the Château Follet, where Alastair once fulfilled her desires.

When just such an opportunity unexpectedly arises, Alastair concedes to her proposition on one condition: that she never again return to Château Follet.

But when their families get together for Christmas and Mildred is confronted with her true feelings for Alastair, will the debauchery of Château Follet prove too great a temptation?

Tempting a Marquess for Christmas

A Super Steamy Regency Romance

By Georgette Brown

Chapter One

MILDRED ABBOTT WINCED AS HER mother emitted a wail of despair. She had no wish to cause her mother pain, but in this, her relief exceeded her guilt.

"You must speak to Haversham again," Mrs. Abbott insisted.

But Mr. Abbott had settled into his favorite armchair before the hearth, and having done so, was unlikely to rise for some time.

"He has decided to depart for Scotland tomorrow."

"All the more reason to speak to him before it is too late," his wife said, her voice high and shrill with desperation.

Mr. Abbott shook his head. "It would do no

good. It is not Haversham who must change his mind. It is Alastair."

Mildred drew in a deep breath. Her cousin had done it. Though he had initially refused to intervene in the matter of her engagement, in the end he had brought about the result she had hoped for. She had erred in accepting Mr. Haversham's proposal, and only the Marquess of Alastair had the position and the influence to alter the arrangement without too much consequence falling upon the formerly engaged couple.

"Surely something can be done," Mrs. Abbott persisted. "Haversham was partial to our Millie. I know it."

"Apparently not enough to acquiesce to the marriage settlements required by Alastair."

Mrs. Abbott wrung her hands. "I know not why the Marquess has decided to concern himself in this matter when he has never concerned himself with us before. Why now?"

"I suppose it is my fault for having approached him with a request for Millie's dowry."

"Nevertheless, he is not the one who need marry Haversham!"

Millie suppressed a smile at the idea of her cousin marrying Haversham. The two men could not be more unalike. The latter was an obsequious dandy who had modest connections, the former was an arrogant and, many deemed, cold-hearted man of quality.

Mr. Abbott reached for his newspaper. "Well, as he is the one providing Millie's dowry, he has a right to interfere."

Mrs. Abbott gave another wail. "Now who will

have Millie? It is not as if she has a queue of men wishing to court her!"

Mildred took no offense at this, for it was true. Though there was much she could yet do to improve her appearance, she knew her beauty to be middling. She had neither soft tresses, long lashes nor the slender figure desired by most. She had other qualities that would serve a husband well, but there was a part of her that few would find acceptable.

Beneath her facade of sense and goodness, churned a dark and prurient nature. She had been much ashamed of this part of her until Alastair's aunt, Lady Katherine, had come across her in a compromising way. In agony that she might have ruined her family, Mildred had been greatly astonished when Lady Katherine had comforted her and, later, *encouraged* her.

It had been an immense relief to Mildred to find that she was not alone in her lustful proclivities, and that these were shared by a woman whom she respected and admired.

"Now Millie will never marry!" Mrs. Abbott lamented as she sank to the sofa.

Mildred took a seat beside her mother and passed her a handkerchief to dab her eyes. Spinsterhood was not a prospect that daunted Mildred, save for the grief that her parents might experience. She was their only child, and as they had but the most modest of means despite their connection to Andre d'Aubigne, Marquess of Alastair, their only hope of seeing their daughter provided for was through marriage. For this reason, Mildred had accepted Haversham's hand.

But regret had set in within minutes of her acceptance. That night, she had decided that she would rather face spinsterhood than marry Haversham. If a husband could not be had—she wondered that she could ever find the right man to marry—she would find employment as a governess or lady's companion. She could appeal for assistance to Lady Katherine, who had taken a liking to her. She would secure her own future.

"I feel quite ill," Mrs. Abbott said.

"Shall I assist you to bed, Mama?" Mildred asked.

"No, no. I am too aggrieved to move."

"Millie's dowry is still in place," Mr. Abbott assured his wife without glancing from his paper. "Alastair has even raised the amount to four thousand pounds. I expect we will see more suitors than we care to entertain."

Mrs. Abbott leaped to her feet. "Four thousand pounds! Truly? Why did you not speak of this first? Why, with such a grand sum, Millie can have much better than Haversham."

Mildred sat, stunned. She had not requested this of Alastair, and she doubted that her father, who had been more than pleased with half the amount, would have dared request more than had been initially granted.

Mrs. Abbott practically danced about the drawing room. "I must tell Mrs. Porter of this! She will not believe it! At last, my brother's marriage to a d'Aubigne has produced some benefit for us. I can almost forgive him now for his lack of consideration. He ought to have provided for the rest of us instead of keeping the riches of the d'Aubigne family to himself."

Mildred said nothing, for Richard, Mrs. Abbott's older brother, had passed away many years ago and was thus beyond receiving her clemency. And Mildred believed that her uncle, perhaps ashamed of his humble background, acted to protect the d'Aubignes from clamoring relatives.

"Richard would have us believe that Alastair had not a generous bone in his body, but at four thousand pounds… Well, I suppose it makes up for his lack of attention to us all these years. It amazes me how little he has done for us. Millie is his cousin, after all."

"By marriage, not blood," Mildred reminded her mother.

"Oh! The difference ought not matter. I had hoped the two of you could have formed a bond as you are not so very different in age."

Mildred flushed. Her mother could never know that, for one night, a special bond *of the most intimate nature* had been had between Mildred and Alastair, but not the sort Mrs. Abbott would have ever conceived.

Mildred pressed her legs tighter together as she recalled how delightfully the Marquess had attended to the flesh between her thighs *with his tongue.* And she, in turn, had taken his member into her mouth. How exquisitely naughty it had all been. How amazingly rapturous.

Mildred had tried not to recall too often her night at Château Follet, nee the Château Debauchery, when she had submitted her body to Alastair. But resistance was futile. It had been the most memorable event of her life. She had replayed every moment, and each recollection produced a heat inside of her. In the quiet of her bedchambers, she had fondled herself to the memories. She had found her own touch wanting compared to his, but she dared not dream for an encore. She still marveled that she had managed to harry him into taking her and fulfilling her deepest, darkest desires.

She had resolved, despite Alastair's belief to the contrary, that how they regarded and interacted with each other would be unchanged.

"You think our relationship can remain the same after what happened?" Alastair had challenged her the morning after their congress.

"Why not?"

"Your naivety is charming at best."

"Well, we are not often in each other's company," she had replied. "The night will hold little significance for you after you have had a tumble with Miss Hollingsworth or whomever you choose next. I daresay you will have forgotten the night altogether after your next visit here."

She wondered if he had forgotten, then told herself that of course he had. She was but one of many whom he, a known rake, had taken to bed, and had done so, undoubtedly, with reluctance.

"I wonder if we should invite Mr. Carleton to dinner?" Mrs. Abbott mused aloud. "I think he could be persuaded to take an interest in Millie, now that her dowry is the sum of four thousand pounds."

"Mr. Carleton!" Mildred shuddered. The man was worse than Haversham.

"His family's merchant business does very well,

I understand."

"He lobbied *against* the abolition of the slave trade."

"He was not the only one, my girl. And do not suppose that you can disparage such prospects simply because you have a dowry of four thousand. Four thousand!" she cried, her voice shrill this time from glee. "Mrs. Porter had thought her nephew too good for the likes of Millie, but she will have to reconsider now that Millie has *four thousand pounds*!"

Mildred frowned. Mrs. Porter's nephew, a portly fellow afflicted by gout and who disdained of bluestockings and the need for women to display their intelligence, was hardly a better prospect than Carleton. This would not do. This would not do at all. She saw a dinner table full of prospective suitors her mother had invited, hours upon hours of making polite conversation with dull-wits and no end to her mother's efforts at matchmaking.

"But I think Mr. Winslow, her neighbor, may also take an interest in Millie. He had been courting Miss Bennett, but I heard she had taken a fancy to some dandy."

"I thought Winslow to be courting Miss Stephenson," Mr. Abbott commented.

"That was *last* year, shortly after he was courting Miss Drury. Or was it Miss Laney he had been partial to?"

Mildred leaped to her feet. "I think I shall go for a walk."

"Alone?" Mr. Abbott inquired, looking up from his paper, perhaps fearing he would be compelled to keep her company, though it was her custom to take solitary walks.

"I may stop to visit Mrs. Bridges," Mildred replied, regretting the necessity to fib. In truth, she intended to pay a visit to her cousin.

"Do not make it a long visit, as dusk will be upon you before you realize."

"Yes, Papa."

As she exited the drawing room, she heard her mother say, "Perhaps I shall take tea with Mrs. Elliott tomorrow. She has a sea captain staying with her. He is quite a bit older than Mildred, and his complexion reminds me of worn leather, but that is to be expected when one spends as many days beneath the sun as he must…"

Mildred threw on a pelisse, quickly pinned on her bonnet, and slipped on her gloves as she hustled out the door. It was no short distance to Grosvenor Square, where Alastair lived, but she was unafraid of walking.

She could not permit Alastair to increase her dowry to such an amount. It was beyond generous, a trait she—or anyone else—would not have expected to exist in the Marquess. What could have possibly prompted such a gesture from him? She doubted her father, who had been quite nervous at requesting a dowry in the first place and would likely not have done it if not for the prodding of his wife, would have ventured to ask for it.

But why would Alastair have volunteered to raise her dowry? Lest his aunt had persuaded him to? Mildred supposed this must be so. Lady Katherine had a kind heart and was partial to Mildred. She would have to thank her ladyship, but they simply could not accept so generous a dowry. Mildred shuddered to think whom else Mrs. Abbott had in store for her.

Mildred quickened her steps. Though she would rather not make any further requests of her cousin, especially when she had exacted quite a bit from him already, she simply had to convince Alastair to rescind the four thousand pounds.

Chapter Two

MILDRED SCANNED THE GAMING HALL looking for her cousin. She spotted him at the faro table flanked on either side by two beauties. The flaxen-haired beauty to his right leaned often toward him, her shoulder grazing his every other minute. The woman to his left had wide rouged lips, and the longest lashes Mildred had ever seen. She batted them at Alastair from behind her ivory-handled fan.

The attentions of the two women did not surprise Mildred, for the Marquess of Alastair had a striking, if not imposing, countenance framed by the d'Aubigne curls of ebony and all the qualities desired in form for his sex: a broad chest, square shoulders, and posture that accentuated his height. Though Mildred had not been struck at first by his handsomeness, for his eyes did not glimmer with charm and he did not often smile, since their encounter at Château Follet, she had come to find him compelling in other ways.

"Please let Lord Alastair know that his cousin

wishes to speak to him," Mildred informed the footman. She could tell the Marquess was engrossed in his game, for he paid the two women beside him little attention. Mildred would not be surprised if he should choose to ignore her request for an audience. His butler, in informing her of his lordship's whereabouts, had warned her that he would not wish to be disturbed. For that reason, Mildred had kept her bonnet and coat.

She drew in a sharp breath as she watched the footman deliver her message to Alastair. Her cousin glanced up from his cards, he seemed neither pleased nor displeased, and Mildred decided it mattered not if he should see her. If he declined, she could always write him a letter expressing her gratitude. Indeed, she wondered at the necessity in coming to deliver her thanks in person. She wondered at her own eagerness. Had it been simply an excuse to see him?

The footman returned, and Mildred braced herself to receive the news that the Marquess was indisposed, but the servant said, "If it pleases you, miss, you may await his lordship in the parlor down the hall."

She released the breath she had been holding and answered, "Yes, of course."

She followed the footman to the parlor. After he had left her alone, she sauntered about the small but nicely appointed broom. She had not the patience to sit upon the sofa in the middle of the room. Why, of a sudden, did she feel nervous? It was silly. She was merely going to thank him.

She had only felt such nerves one other time with her cousin. It was the night she had approached him at his aunt Katherine's birthday to request his assistance in getting out of her engagement with Haversham. She did not often find him as intimidating as others would.

But there was no denying that the nature of their relationship had changed since that fateful night at the Château Debauchery. Not only had she lifted her skirts to him, she had done so in the most wanton fashion.

To keep her mind from straying into the past, she studied the baroque longcase clock in the corner, wandered to the hearth to warm her gloved hands at the fire, and viewed herself in the looking glass above the mantel. She was glad she was comely enough such that Alastair had capitulated to her desires. She had fancied that perhaps he had even desired her a little, enough to be aroused, though she had heard that his sex required little in the way of arousal and could be titillated by the prospect of congress with any woman, even if she was not the most striking.

"What is amiss?"

She whirled about to face her cousin. Now that he was in closer proximity, he appeared more imposing. She tried not to recall how strong and heavy his body had felt against her.

"Nothing," she answered, gratified that his voice had carried more concern than was his custom.

"Then why are you here, Millie?"

Now he sounded displeased.

"I came first to thank you," she said, refusing to be intimidated by his mood. "Father said that Haversham departs for Scotland on the morrow."

"Good riddance. May I suggest that you pick

your next husband more carefully?"

"Of course. I rather think that I shall not be accepting any more proposals for some time."

He made no reply, and she suspected that he desired to return to the card tables, but she could not leave without addressing her other request.

"I would have written a letter to express my heartfelt thanks, but I was uncertain when it would reach you, and I did not think that it would have adequately communicated the sincerity of my gratitude."

"No thanks are necessary."

Knowing the best manner of thanks she could provide at the moment was allowing him to return to his cards, and perhaps the two beauties that awaited him, Mildred could not resist staying him for just a minute. "But you will have it, nonetheless, for it is the proper and polite response to express gratitude where it is due."

"And when have you known me to care for what is proper and polite?"

She grinned. "*I* will do what is right and bestow my thanks. *You* may choose to receive it however you wish."

"Consider yourself acquitted of any further obligation. What is your second reason for coming, and I daresay I hope there is not a third?"

"Worry not. I do not plan to keep you long, and you may return to your vices soon. I have but a simple request."

He raised his brows. "Another request?"

She flushed, realizing she had imposed upon him rather often of late. "It shall be my last."

"I pray it so or it might become a habit."

Ignoring his rudeness, she forged on. "I should dearly appreciate it if you were to return my dowry to the original amount of two thousand pounds—or even less."

He stared at her.

"I know not what my father might have said," she continued, "but two thousand pounds was more than kind."

He crossed his arms. "Never before have I encountered anyone whom it is so difficult to bestow money to. You spoke of what is proper and polite. It would be proper and polite of you to accept my donation and be grateful for it."

"I am grateful for your generosity but would not encroach upon it further."

"Alas, it is not for you to do so. Your father has accepted the new dowry on behalf of your family."

"Well, of course he did!"

"Because anyone of middling intelligence would."

She drew in a sharp breath, then saw a glimmer in his eyes that allowed her to release her breath. "Alastair, you have been more than kind, but four thousand pounds is beyond the pale. I do not merit such a sum."

"There are plenty of unworthy women with far larger dowries than you."

She suppressed a scowl. "But why the need to increase the amount?"

"Because you merit better than Haversham."

"But four thousand pounds will attract every Tom, Dick and Harry."

"That is not my problem, Millie."

"But you—" She forced herself to take a breath. How the man tried her civility!

"You are a clever girl. I expect you will learn the art of rejecting your suitors without badly wounding their hearts—or pride."

"I've no wish to. Dealing with Haversham was enough for me."

"Millie, you have made several requests of me, and I have no desire to encourage further requests from you. Thus, my answer is *no*."

Her mouth hung agape before she landed upon another strategy. "If that is your position, then you shall have to suffer my gratitude and many, many expressions of it—and often—profusely—for such a level of generosity deserves praise and—"

To her surprise, he drew up before her, and the air surrounding them suddenly constricted.

"Are you threatening me?" he growled.

Her heart palpitated rapidly. His proximity left her without words. Though she had told herself that one too many glasses of wine at the Chateau Debauchery had contributed to the amorous affect her cousin had upon her, the truth was rather different, as evidenced by the melting sensation she currently felt.

Seeing that he had silenced her, he retreated a pace. "Are we done, Millie?"

Never had gathering words proved so difficult, but she managed a "yes."

Pulling her shawl tighter about her, she made for the doors.

"Wait."

The command sent her hurling back to that night at Château Follett, when she had followed his directives in delicious delight. Her heart still beating rapidly, she dared not look at him, not wanting him to see the effect he had upon her.

"How did you arrive?" he inquired.

She turned around only after she had enough composure in hand. "I walked here by foot."

He looked toward the window. The skies outside had begun to darken. "The hour is late. You should take my carriage."

"Thank you for the offer, but I am not daunted by the distance home."

"Did you come alone?"

"Yes, but—"

"Then you will take my carriage."

"I enjoy walking."

The cool air would help dampen the warmth swirling inside her.

He gave her a penetrating stare, and for a moment, she thought he might finish the thought he'd had earlier and specify a punishment for her refusal. She shivered at such a prospect. "I will not require my carriage for some time," he said, removing any last obstacle to her acceptance. "Time enough for my driver to take you home and return."

"Very well," she declared. Then, wanting to reclaim a little of her pride, she dared to irk him. "I accept your hospitality. Let it not be said that the Marquess of Alastair lacks kindness."

His countenance darkened, and he grumbled, "Consider yourself fortunate, Millie, that we are *not* at Château Follett."

His words took her breath once more. She wanted a ready retort but could not conjure one.

She watched him open the doors and call to a footman to have his carriage ready.

"Good night, Millie," Alastair said before heading back to the card room.

She was glad he did not tarry to keep her company while she waited for his carriage. His presence rattled her more than she liked. Now that he had mentioned Château Follett, there was no holding back from venturing there in her mind.

Tempting a Marquess for Christmas
Available November 2017

For further reading, check out:

WORKS BY GEORGETTE BROWN

STEAMY REGENCY COLLECTION
An Indecent Wager (Book #1)
Surrendering to the Rake (Book #2)
That Wicked Harlot (Book #3)
Tempting a Marquess (Book #4)
Tempting a Marquess for Christmas (Book #5)

OTHER
Pride, Prejudice & Pleasure